Hell's Mirror

by

DeAnna Davidson Lipps

The contents of this work including, but not limited to, the accuracy of events, people, and places depicted; opinions expressed; permission to use previously published materials included; and any advice given or actions advocated are solely the responsibility of the author, who assumes all liability for said work and indemnifies the publisher against any claims stemming from publication of the work.

The names and places used in this novel are strictly coincidental.

All Rights Reserved
Copyright © 2019 by DeAnna Davidson Lipps

No part of this book may be reproduced or transmitted, downloaded, distributed, reverse engineered, or stored in or introduced into any information storage and retrieval system, in any form or by any means, including photocopying and recording, whether electronic or mechanical, now known or hereinafter invented without permission in writing from the publisher.

Dorrance Publishing Co
585 Alpha Drive
Suite 103
Pittsburgh, PA 15238
Visit our website at www.dorrancebookstore.com

ISBN: 978-1-6442-6654-0
eISBN: 978-1-6442-6673-1

ACKNOWLEDMENTS

Special Thanks: Don and Cora Davidson, Tony Lipps, Tim and Marlene Hanner, Pam Park, Bobby and Glenda Garnett, Melinda Johnson, Lynn Forman, Leaha Franks, Mellissa Huff, Robert Otte, Phil Berne, Rodney Vivian, Tim Mitchell, Sharon Lipps, Margaret Hoffman, Rose Mary Hoffman, Kay Langdon, C.M.

For all of you who shine brighter than the sun; you bring hope in the dark.

Special Thanks: Dorrance Publishing Co. for helping me so much throughout this process. It has been wonderful to work with Dorrance in all aspects of this novel.

To my mother and father
(the two most wonderful people in the world)

To my husband, Tony
(my love and my heart song)

To C.M., J.P., M.H., and G.G.
(who helped light the way)

"Darkness is not the absence of light; it's the absence of hope."

Hell's Mirror

Are you willing to look
In the mirror at last
What does it reflect.
"A heart of future past"

One that is kind
Fights the good fight
Stands ever proudly
And, lives in the light.

Might a shadow
Be hiding in there.
Lurking about
For a victim to snare.

For in his darkness
Floating below
Greedily taking
An offered-up soul.

With a nod of his head
Like a pull from a string.
His demons will fly
Upon feathered wing.

And, when he grasps you
In his fiery hand,
Beware, beware
Your soul may be damned.

Fight against
This **Hell** on earth.
The afterlife
Will be much worse.

Stay true to the power
That fights the night.
And, "rage against
The dying of the light."

Because, one thing is certain
One thing is clear.
There will come a day
When we all face **The Mirror.**

Chapter One
Revenge Is a Dish Best Served Cold
Present Day

Every year it came like a wildfire burning over the landscape, raging over his body like lava in his soul, burning, ripping and tearing. He remembered when he was much younger. When the leaves were crunchy and falling to the ground like they did year after year. The nights were getting a bit cooler and he and his friends talked about what costumes they might be wearing for one of their most favorite nights of the year. They would carry pillowcases from house to house, running with that wonderful phrase, "Trick or treat!" Then, moving on to another house using that phrase again and again. The night filled with excitement to see what kind of candy they might get next.

Such a happy time in their lives. The night alive with laughter. Someone might jump out and growl or yell "BOO" with a scary costume to make Halloween a little more festive. And the other children might jump at the thrill of being scared and that would make them laugh even more. A real honest-to-goodness belly laugh. The kind of laugh that made you double over and hold your stomach until it ached. Those belly laughs were one of the best things in the entire world. They were pure glee! As soon as one ended, another one would begin. What a glorious time to be young, alive, and free on that amazing night of nights, along with the sounds and the smells that came along with All Hallows' Eve.

The fall wind carried scents of pumpkin pie that some of the homes had made and it floated through the air like a promise of the future. The crisp, tasty caramel apples made by Mrs. Connor wafted in the air. As they trotted along in the cool mist, the sights and sounds of autumn were everywhere on those Halloween nights when he and his friends were young and carefree. It was almost like a movie scene that had been created just for them as they walked through the little town, all of them happy to be together and enjoy another spooky night in their lives. So amazing because they all knew the pure happiness that came with the mystical wonderland of magic all around them.

Going from house to house, they received one prize after another: popcorn balls, Snickers, bubblegum, Nestlé Crunch, Blow Pops, Kit Kats, Milky Way, Almond Joy, Mounds, Tootsie Rolls, Hershey Bars, caramel apples, Butterfingers, lollipops, and always a toothbrush handed out from the local dentist, Mr. Fletcher.

Mr. Granger, who owned the small store in town, gave out the big-sized candy bars. Everyone stopped at the Grangers' each year. Their pillowcases were always full of candy when they finally headed home.

Oh, and who could forget *It's the Great Pumpkin, Charlie Brown*? All of his friends would watch it together every year and they laughed when Charlie "got a rock each time." Charlie was a "lovable loser" and they laughed about the rocks, but they loved him all the same. Because in every Charlie Brown cartoon, there was always a happy ending for Charlie and his friends.

And, the beautiful pottery they made every year in Mrs. Huff's room was amazing! She was the art teacher and always came up with something wonderful at Halloween that was spectacular to create. One year her class crafted the cutest little ghost, white with big green eyes. All of them came out great. Then the class created a song about the ghost. Mrs. Huff was a music teacher as well and she played the piano. The song had to rhyme and everyone contributed to their very own class song. That year it was called "Ghost Rockin' Eve."

Then just as suddenly as the memories came they were gone as he stood at the window watching the trees. He saw that the leaves were turning red and a golden brown. The town was getting ready for Halloween. But this year the most ultimate game would be played on All Hallows' Eve. His plan was ready. He had worked on it for so many years and this Halloween he would put his plan into motion. He had waited for the right time to bring justice to the town of River's Edge, striking with a cold and calculated brand of his own. He felt like the pain had been stitched on his body like a never-ending tattoo, never letting go. So much pain living inside of him for so long. It had taken a long time to follow through with his plan, and now All Hallows' Eve would have all the festivities that they did every year with one more trick.

May God have mercy on their souls! Because, he had none. He knew he was probably bound for Hell. But, by God, he would take them with him. Every last one.

One name printed in the middle of all seven envelopes. The wildfire still burning, raging inside his body. He placed the envelopes inside the pocket of his long black coat. He walked outside, ready to put the plan in motion. They will never see me coming.

There would be no happy ending in River's Edge this year. He would make sure of that, creating his own reality for the players in his long-awaited game.

As he walked to his car the sky held a thunderstorm about to come on strong. But, it was nothing like what he had planned for the town. "For, **I am the storm**," he whispered with a profound sense of truth. And, when he said the words out loud they solidified the hell that awaited all seven members of a group that use to call themselves *the shit* when they were teenagers. They were now going to reap what they had sewn so many years ago.

Chapter Two

The Town

Twenty-five Years Ago, All Hallows' Eve

The kids ran hooting and hollering down the streets of the river town. It looked as if most of the people living in the center of doom were on a paint strike; cracked and brittle houses stood withering in the chilly wind like a ramshackle village that was left to crash and burn. However, during the holidays the town always felt different. The gleaming lights and decorations made the place less gloomy. It gave hope to the people of River's Edge. But, when all festivities were over, it once again became one of the most dismal places in the world.

The town of River's Edge, Kentucky, sat right above the banks of the Ohio River. That was one good thing about the town. Although the river ran right below the banks, it never flooded because the town was high above the water's edge. Other towns farther down the banks of the river were not as lucky. However, for River's Edge, it still seemed as though it was beginning to rot. That was a good word for the dank and dingy streets that made up the inner town of River's Edge. A better name for this shabby wasteland might be "Oppression". For that was how the town felt. Even as children they could feel it seeping deep into their skin like a chronic disease.

The outskirts of the depressing landscape gave way to finer homes. But the infestation of what some people might call the devil dwelt within the confines of the city limits and had begun to grow like a cancerous tumor, which had metastasized with tendrils of hate and horror woven throughout the decomposing mass.

Evil had come to call on River's Edge. It grew within the unmown grass and weeds in so many of the yards, lacing its darkly formed fingers in the peeling paint of the poorer families. Choking the houses of the wealthy that felt safe in the comfort that money could bring, finding its way into the homes of the people who were unfortunate enough to live in a town that was *headed for Hell in a handbasket*.

The town had one grocery store on Front Street that overlooked the grayish river. It stocked staple items like candy and different flavors of soda pop. Mr. and Mrs. Granger lived above the store and ran a relatively good business. They allowed the folks of River's Edge to run a tab and pay at the end of each month.

River's Edge Elementary and Middle School sat right in the middle of the gloom-laden town. It housed first through ninth grades. There was one class per grade level with the numbers ranging from ten to twenty students per class. It was painted a pale green color and there were no bright posters that adorned the classroom walls. It was as crippled and broken as the town. This festering boil of a building loomed like an iridescent monster in which the evil was born.

River's Edge Baptist Church sat right next door to the school. It was painted white but years of wear and tear on the old building left it looking as tarnished as the river.

What were considered to be the "good folk" of River's Edge went to church every time the doors were open. Reverend Happer was a fire-and-brimstone type of preacher. If you came to church feeling like a good Christian that morning, you had a great uncertainty of that fact as you walked out the door that afternoon!

The Sunday school teachers were all devout gossipers. They spent the meetings that were to be used in planning *Bible* lessons for the children, talking about anyone and everyone that might have a juicy story unfolding in their lives. The latest scandal to rock the town was about Anthony Preston III. His wife had left him several years ago and he was supposedly banging anyone in a skirt.

Of course, at that time, the Sunday school ladies had no idea that one of their group was hiking up her *own skirt* every time Anthony Preston wanted a roll in the hay. Lou Ella Armstrong, ten years married with two children, taught second grade *Bible* lessons every Sunday morning. Every Sunday night, after evening services, Lou Ella met Anthony Preston III in his shiny red Cadillac Convertible for a different kind of lesson.

Yes, you might say that River's Edge, Kentucky, was like a lot of little towns all over the world; made up of the poor and the wealthy, the righteous as well as the sinners, the lonely, the needy, the honest and the dishonest, the movers and the shakers, the gossips and the do-gooders. Filled with small houses, big houses, poor houses, wealthy houses, a school, a church, a store, a restaurant, a power and electric company, a gas station, and a small bank. River's Edge might be considered to be the perfect town in which the devil could creep down the streets and send out an invitation to come out and play.

Chapter Three

THE PACK

TWENTY-FIVE YEARS AGO, ALL HALLOWS' EVE

The group of seven thirteen-year-olds raced down the sidewalks, bent on having a bit of Halloween fun. They were *the shit!* And if anyone knew about shit, it was the group of yipping street urchins running hilly-nilly hither and yon through the streets of River's Edge. They had egged the Grangers' store windows, watching as bright bubbles of yellow splayed across the dirty glass.

"That was *the shit!*" Ernie yelled as the other kids grinned and agreed with nods of the head and howls of laughter. "*the shit*" was a term that Ernie came up with a few weeks ago and now he used the expression for all devilish acts they considered to be rude, crude, and violent.

Ernie had golden coppery hair and perfectly straight huge, white teeth. He was the epitome of a bully with a capital "B." He was feared and ruled with an air of brazen audacity even at such a young age. Along with this high and mighty personality was a slick and crafty brain. He was as smart as he was venomous. And that was a deadly combination for the town.

His parents were drunks, living like doped-out slugs over eighty percent of the time. Ernie always turned up with bruises on his face. Although none of *the pack* ever mentioned it, they knew he was a battered boy.

"We are *the shit!*" crooned Todd Barker at the top of his lungs.

This produced another infectious laugh from the rest of the six hoodlums.

Todd Barker came from one of the more prominent homes. It stood on the outskirts of town in which the paint strike had not been heralded as of yet. His parents were both doctors and worked at the clinic outside of River's Edge. Todd called them do-gooders and vowed he would never become a damned do-gooder. He hated his parents with a passion. Of course, he was as sweet as pickled jam in their presence. His mother still believed he was her little Toddy Woddy. It was an easy show to pull off for old Todd because it was his brown-haired, blue-eyed, boyish good looks that allowed him to get away with murder. But, Toddy Woddy was long gone, replaced by the mean spirit of a thirteen-year-old who wanted to show Ernie he was as bad assed as him.

"Good one, Ernie!" yelled Ray White.

"Good one, Ernie!" mimicked Todd in a girlish voice. "You're so gay! Get away from me, fag bag!" Todd pushed Ray, and he fell flat on his pudgy little baby face.

Ray's face turned red as blood. He was the bottom feeder of *the pack*. His pudgy size made him an easy target for the rest of the group. They all knew how much Ray wanted to be liked, so they kept him around to have a little fun at Gay Ray's expense. He was weak; *the pack* capitalized on that fact and used him for entertainment value only.

Ray raised himself up on his knees and began to clean his glasses with a spare hanky he kept in his back pocket for an occasion such as this. His glasses were always spiraling off his face one way or another. If someone didn't push him down, shove him across the room, ram him up against the locker, or just run into him on purpose, his glasses still needed cleaning at least ten times a day. He knew his face was red as an apple after being treated like that by Todd, but Ray wanted nothing more than to hang with this group that ruled the school. It was beginning to win him some leverage with some of the other boys and they were beginning to leave him alone. Because when they saw Ray with Ernie, all the other boys who were thought of as bullies backed away. Everyone was scared shitless of Ernie Johnson, and to be considered one of his friends was like living royalty at River's Edge Elementary. So, Ray let *the pack* tease him. In his way of thinking, it was better to be one of them than to face the school alone.

His father was the local sheriff in town. Both of his parents had high expectations that Ray would follow in his father's shoes. But if Ray didn't grow a pair in the next few years, his father could wash that dream right down *the shitter*.

Vera Tate gave Gay Ray a shove with her sneaker so that he found himself nose to nose with the pavement again.

"I'm so bored!" Vera said. "These are little kiddie pranks. When are we going to have some *real* fun?"

Vera was the mouth of *the pack*. They called her "Mouth" because she was so loud and obnoxious. Vera got that honestly from her mother. A woman who talked out of both sides of her *own mouth*, into which she also stuffed large amounts of food. Pretty soon she wasn't going to be able to fit through the door of *Buster's Burgers and Fries*, where she worked as a slow, sloppy waitress.

Ms. Tate had worked at the restaurant in Pineville, the next town over, for the last twenty years. *Buster's Burgers and Fries* served pretty decent food. Patrons came from many surrounding communities, including the local riffraff. They ran a good business. The vile-rooted infection had not made its way into their restaurant, as of yet. Although, at times you could smell it in the air like a decaying animal.

The rest of *the pack* included three more townies. The Happer twin boys were as cunning and as ruthless as the rest. With white-yellow hair and pulsating blue eyes, John and Paul Happer were named after disciples. What a joke. They were cruel, calculating animals who preyed on the weaknesses of others.

Their father was the local minister at the River's Edge Baptist Church. Every Sunday the Happer twins sat in the front pew in matching suits, thinking only about the next time they could meet up with *the pack*.

Sitting with them at these church functions was Tabitha Preston. The last but not the least member of the group who thought they were *"the shit."* She was a beauty with her chestnut hair and violet eyes, but looks could be deceiving.

Tabitha's family was rich. They lived in the biggest house, had the finest cars, and all the best things that money could buy. And they never let anyone forget it for one minute. Her father, Anthony Preston III, had inherited the money from his great-grandfather. They had old money, Tabitha said. For some reason Tabitha thought old money was way better than new money.

"Vera's right!" Todd piped up as the night began to get colder. "Let's do some real damage. Fuck this egg throwing."

Ernie smiled through his Chiclet teeth. The rest of *the pack* whooped and hollered as they moved on down Second Street. A presence of darkness hissed at their heels and wove its way in between their bodies. No doubt about it, *they were the shit*!

Coming Together

The members of *the pack* came together as if drawn by a force of nature. The tornado whipping at their backs pushed them into a chasm as black and deep as the depths of hell itself. The storm rocking and plundering their souls became a trap in which none of them could escape—a violent, unstoppable beast, growing in intensity year after year.

Charging into the fray of the town like a monster; spinning, whirling, hurling through space and time. As if an asteroid of the cosmos was pummeling forward and leaving a trail of fire and ash in its wake. Wreaking havoc and pain on the inhabitants of River's Edge, *the pack reigned supreme*. Their broken and splintered personalities formed a bond that would eventually be sealed by the blood of the innocent.

Chapter Four
The Beginning of the End
Present Day

Ernie Johnson Sr. looked outside as the rain began to fall. It was a light rain, but soon it would be a flat-out thunderstorm. A bolt of lightning streaked across the sky as if to remind him of the power of nature. Ernie didn't need reminding. He knew all about the power of nature.

Beaten and broken as a child, he fought back the only way he knew how. Control. He ruled over his employees with an iron fist. He berated them every time a chance was provided, because Ernie knew well that was how to keep control over other weak-minded people who desperately needed their jobs. Yes, Ernie had done all right for himself in River's Edge. He was now in charge of the Preston Power and Electric Company.

However, the job had come with its share of obedience. There was only one reason Ernie was in charge of the power plant and that was Tabitha Preston. Ernie seethed inside knowing the true "power" Tabitha had over who he had become. Once poor and desperate, he now had the money to buy the whole damn town. Although Tabitha would not give up her name when they married, he had still managed to become the head of *his* household.

His parents both died when he was eighteen and Ernie was not sorry to see them go. In a drunken frenzy his father had shot his mother and killed himself. He was relieved when the slobbering drunks finally met their end.

They were stupid people. Ernie was a true genius and had no idea how two slobbering drunks could have had a child like him. He had the highest IQ in the entire town. But he had learned one thing from his parents: Domination could be achieved if you were smart, not stupid as a dumbass piece of shit. And in this town, he ruled supreme.

As Ernie turned from the window the front door burst open. His two sons came running through the door. Ernie Jr., who had just turned thirteen, and Evan, an exuberant nine-year-old who was a namby-pamby pain in the ass from the time he was born. He cried at the drop of a hat when something hurt his feelings and Ernie felt the need to beat it out of him. But, Tabitha had put a stop to that right away.

Ernie Jr. was his pride and joy. The spitting image of his father in more ways than one. Ernie Jr. knocked Evan on the side of the head as they walked into the kitchen. He was a spunky boy who would eventually own the business. Ernie Sr. smiled at that notion. The Johnson name would someday take the place of Preston on the power and electric company. As soon as Tabitha's father kicked the bucket, he would take complete control.

"Hey, Dad, brought the mail. It's going to be a thunderstorm from hell," Ernie Jr. quipped.

"Ernie, Mom says 'hell' is a bad word," said Evan.

"You go to hell," smirked Ernie Jr.

Evan began to tear up and Ernie Sr. had to suppress an eye roll that carried with it disgust for his younger son.

"Get upstairs and do your homework, both of you. And take off those wet shoes before you track mud all over the house."

Ernie Jr. left the mail on the counter as he and Evan headed up to their rooms. The thirteen-year-old for a bullying session on the computer and Evan to complete his assignment like a good little boy.

As Ernie Sr. reached for the mail he felt a shiver run up his spine. It was as if the devil himself was standing in the room with him. The white envelope in his hand had his name typed across the back. His address was not listed nor was there a return address. He opened it and took out the folded paper and stared at the seven words typed neatly in the center of the page. *This is the beginning of your end.*

Chapter Five
Seven Envelopes
Present Day

The plan was in motion. He'd placed his envelopes in the mailboxes of the five houses. Two of them were located in the prominent section of Preston. Well-maintained yards that could not hide the decay that began many years ago. Wealth didn't matter in this game. Hadn't they all proved that fact? Evil could take root in the rich houses as well as the poor. It could manifest within the insanely religious as well as the begotten. Both were subject to Satan's power and when you invited him in, God have mercy on your soul.

The other three homes looked as if a small gust of wind would blow them down. The shabby dwellings were a testament to the pain and suffering of the world; they looked as ragged as they did twenty-five years ago.

He walked to his car and shielded his body from the thunderstorm that was in full swing. Lightning flashed and the thunder rolled. It was the perfect night to be concealed by the veil of darkness provided by a starless sky. A smile played across his face; it was the perfect night for the game to begin. He pulled away from the last house and drove home thinking about what would be occurring in each house this very evening. It would have been wonderful to be there when each of them opened those envelopes. So he pictured it in his mind. And, that alone was satisfying—very satisfying, indeed!

Chapter Six
I Must Win! I Must Win!
Present Day

Vera stared at the words printed on the stark white paper. *This is the beginning of your end.* Her stomach and chest burned with the acid making its way to her throat. Stress always made the attacks worse.

She had just gotten home from her shift at *Bob's Burger Palace*, which had recently changed its name from *Buster's Burgers and Fries*. Buster's son, Bob, had taken over the establishment and thought his name would look better on the sign that proclaimed they served the best burger in town. More like the only burger in town.

Settling down to read the mail before fixing dinner for her mother, she slowly sipped a glass of wine hoping it would ease the ache in her bones.

Vera played the *Publishers Clearing House Sweepstakes* consistently. *You can't win if you don't enter* was their slogan. And Vera Tate thought these were the truest words she had ever heard spoken.

She was hoping for another entry form when her eyes fell upon a white envelope with her name typed boldly across the back. She had hesitated only a second before tearing it open and reading the words that now flashed through her mind. It took her back to that night so long ago. Memories that she had shoved under her soul. Ones that she chose not to remember because they were so horrid. Now they hit her like a brick wall. Washing over her like the thunderstorm that was pummeling outside her window.

Staring into space, Vera teetered on the brink of vomiting her lunch back up on the kitchen table. The greasy taste of the burger and fries lingered in her mouth and in her nostrils. Then for a moment, she lost all sense of time. The only thought she had in her mind was *I must win...I must...I must...Then, I can run away from this meager existence.* How wonderful it would be to travel around the world! But, those seven words had taken away the last hope of any kind of happiness, traveling or winning *The Publishers Clearing House Sweepstakes.* All of her dreams were gone. Their secret had been discovered. It was over.

"Vera, what are doing in there so long?" Ms. Tate yelled.

Her mother lay sprawled on the bed as usual watching the soap opera channel. Right now, Erica Cane seemed to be wooing a young man into her bed.

"What is it, Ma?"

"You stupid cow, I've been calling you for thirty minutes," Martha Tate admonished her daughter with a look of disdain. Ms. Tate was now over four hundred pounds and had a hard time getting out of bed. Her days were spent watching soap operas and ordering Vera around when she wasn't working at the restaurant.

As Vera stood in the doorway, she knew it was a picture of what she would be someday. Only she would not have a daughter to order around like a slave. She had never married and was on her way to the two-hundred-pound mark on the bathroom scale. And she was smart enough to know that Prince Charming didn't go for fat women.

"I'm hungry," her mother bristled. "Get the dinner started before I starve to death."

As Vera headed back toward the kitchen to start dinner her thoughts delved into the deep waters of a tortured soul. If only the fat old hag would kick the bucket, Vera might be free to live her life.

But the seven words solidified that would never happen.

Vera Tate stepped into the kitchen remembering that night from all those years ago. Halloween night, to be exact. The vision that clouded her thoughts made her heart race with an all-consuming dread: *This is the beginning of your end.* A reckoning was coming for them. The fire licking at her feet was growing strong and fast with those words and she would burn for what she had done, what all of them had done...burn...burn...burn.

Before she even made it to the stove, Vera passed out deader than a doornail.

Chapter Seven

The End of innocence

Twenty-five Years Ago, All Hallows' Eve

Madeline Singer, Reese Stone, and Brian Caster strolled through the streets of River's Edge with their bags of candy. They all knew that thirteen was a bit old for trick-or-treating, but none of them really wanted to let go of their childhood so soon.

A misty fog was in the air that night. It seemed to go along with the spooky presence of Halloween. They walked a little more slowly. Talked and belly laughed as they always did when they were together. Such great friends they had become. *The Three Musketeers*, as they liked to call themselves, were together every minute time would allow. They had been friends for so long now and the bond was strong. From the first day in first grade when Brian made his name plate all wrong, which Madeline and Reese helped him fix; that was the beginning of a beautiful friendship for all of them.

When Madeline looked back on the memory, she was so glad Brian had made that mistake. If he hadn't maybe they wouldn't be here walking down the streets talking, laughing like only true friends are able to do. And, on this Halloween night she knew how lucky she was to have them. Then she really looked at their costumes and began to giggle.

Reese and Brian had dressed up like zombies. They were passionate about Michael Jackson and thought *Thriller* was the greatest song of all time. The video was what they called *the bomb!*

Madeline had decided to wear a white princess gown. She thought it might be the last time it would be appropriate to wear a princess costume, as she was now leaving her childhood behind.

"Hey, let's race!" shouted Reese. His goal was to impress Madeline with his running ability. It seemed that his crush on her grew more profound every year. His black hair had gray streaks running through it, completing his Halloween costume, and his brown eyes lit up his face when he smiled.

"Yeah, first one to Front Street wins!" Brian shouted.

"But my dress, a princess should never run in a dress," she said as she tucked her long blonde hair behind her ear and laughed at the exuberance of her friends. Her blue eyes twinkled as Reese and Brian got ready to run.

Brian counted to three and he and Reese ran with knees and arms pumping toward Front Street. Reese beat Brian by an inch and couldn't wait to tell Madeline of the victory. They waited on Front Street near the muddy banks that led to the river.

Five minutes stretched into ten. Ten minutes stretched to fifteen. Soon they had waited twenty minutes, but Madeline did not come walking down the street in her princess costume.

"Do you think she's hiding?" Brian said finally, running his hand through his brown hair.

"Maybe she is going to jump out and give us a good scare!" Reese shouted into the moaning wind.

But Madeline did not jump out and Reese started to have a queasy feeling in his gut.

"Maybe she went on home," Brian said hopefully, but something felt wrong as the words rang against his ears.

Worry began to writhe its way through his stomach, and like Reese he started to feel uneasy about Madeline. His light green eyes tried to see as far as they could, down the street where they had begun their race, but he didn't couldn't see her anywhere.

The boys shouted her name. They split up and walked from Front Street to Third Street calling her name, over and over.

CHAPTER EIGHT

DARKNESS

PRESENT DAY

After sealing the fate of *the pack*, he sat alone in his car. He let the darkness wash over him. The shadows moved across his vision again, but he focused with all his might to remember every detail of that Halloween night twenty-five years ago.

It was the screaming that sent him over the edge every time. Those screams that made him seek out the burning liquid that would numb him from the past, if only for a little while. But, as he had become one with the plan that began to form in his mind many years ago, he steeled himself from the alcohol. A clear head would be needed for the game he intended to play. He must be the master chess player if he wanted to win.

The decorations hung from the trees. River's Edge was getting ready for the festivities of *All Hallows' Eve*. His "tricks" would be added to the list this year. Revenge can be a powerful motivator. Letting the anger pulsate through his body, he wondered if the devil now lived within him as he lived within the town.

The screams grew louder, to the point that he thought his head might explode. They burst into a thousand fragments, each holding a picture from his memory of that fateful night when hell descended on the town of River's Edge.

Chapter Nine

The Unimaginable

Twenty-five Years Ago, All Hallows' Eve

A countless number of children passed beneath the body hanging from the tree. In their minds it was just another Halloween decoration to cast a spell of Halloween fun. When the screaming began, no one understood the terror that sprang from the voices of the children. Heart-wrenching cries that would haunt the people of the town forever.

It was complete chaos all around the tree. Older children were trying to console the younger ones to no avail. They were crowded around the tree screaming at a fever pitch, staring up at the body that swayed from the tree. More children gathered and realized what they were seeing and began to cry as someone realized it was Madeline, because of her costume. Then it went from bad to worse. Some of them ran home. Others were in shock. A few of the other teenagers climbed the tree and used a knife to try and sever the rope.

As the first adults arrived upon the scene, they realized the children had in fact found the body of Madeline Singer. Soon sirens could be heard in every direction. When the police arrived they had to rope off the area, which was very hard to do with so many children crying around the tree. When they finally got everything under control, they used the yellow tape to rope of the crime scene. It glowed and fluttered in the wind.

When Madeline's parents arrived, they had to be dragged away from the tree. Tormented and broken, they clung to each other for dear life and asked the same question over and over again: *Why?*

Brian was in the worst shock of his young life. He stood watching the scene unfold before his eyes. Madeline was hanging from a tree? He couldn't speak, he couldn't scream, he couldn't even cry. This just couldn't be real. Any minute now he was going to wake up and it would all be a dream. He stood there staring at the people around him, believing it could not be true. His mother was holding him close and tears were running down her face. Then he saw Reese running toward the tree.

He watched as the police officers were dragging him away kicking and screaming. But he didn't ask *why* this had happened to their sweet and beautiful friend like all the adults that had gathered there on that horrible night. He and Reese both knew why. Children are always the first to recognize when evil is living among them.

After

No one was arrested for the murder of Madeline Singer. People went into their houses and tried to shut themselves off from the horror that lived in the world. Even the police closed the investigation right away. They blamed it on a drifter that must have preyed on the town of River's Edge. A ruthless child killer that would someday be brought to justice in another place and time. They said God would have his revenge upon this Devil.

The people eventually went on with their day-to-day lives while a murderer lurked beneath the shadows of the town.

Chapter Ten
The Do-gooder
Present Day

Dr. Todd Barker sat with his feet up on the couch. He wanted to watch a bit of mind-numbing TV before bed. *Two and a Half Men* provided Todd as much comfort as the tumbler of vodka that sat on the antique table in front of him.

Despite his vow of never becoming like his parents, Todd had followed right in their footsteps. He'd gone to college and then medical school. After marrying, Todd moved back to River's Edge and took over the local clinic when his parents retired. He'd had no intention of ever moving back to the desolate town. But despite his intentions something had pulled him back like an irresistible force of nature. *Atonement?* Was he looking for the peace that deep down he knew he would never find? For that Halloween night so long ago had never left his mind. What they did twenty-five years ago had haunted him like it was yesterday. When those memories came back, sometimes his hands would shake so violently he could barely control them. Especially when the flashbacks came and invaded every crevice of his mind. Sometimes he would need to leave the patient he was attending to just get the attacks under control.

He was a do-gooder now. Something he vowed he would never be as a thirteen-year-old shithead. His wife, Amy, was a doctor as well, and they worked six days a week helping the folks of River's Edge with all of their ailments. There were even some patients that he attended with no charge. It was what his parents had done when they were the family practitioners of the town. They had worked tirelessly for the people of River's Edge. Sometimes he wondered if they had felt the need for *atonement* as well.

His daughter was now a teenager. It had been a tough decision to bring her to the small town and give up the big city life. But in the end, his need for repentance had won the battle.

Two and a Half Men had succeeded in providing an escape along with the vodka. Then, he made the mistake of looking through the mail. His handsome young face suddenly took on the quality of a very old man. The seven words, *This is the beginning of your end*, turned his blood to ice and Old Toddy Woddy wished to God he had never set foot back in the town of River's Edge, Kentucky.

Chapter Eleven

The Sheriff

Present Day

Ray White had also followed in his father's footsteps, though many people thought it would never happen. Even Ray was shocked as hell when he won the election after his father retired. The sheriff had come a long way from his Gay Ray days. However, Gay Ray was hiding a secret. He was gay. He'd known from the time he was ten years old and would have rather played dress-up than roughhouse with the other boys.

By the time he was eleven, he had manifested a deep affection for Todd Barker. He suspected Todd sensed the truth. That Ray was gay and that was the reason Todd had been the one in *the pack* who'd treated him the worst.

Of course, that didn't keep him from following them around like a whipped puppy dog. They treated him like dog shit, but he kept going back for more. He turned the paper over and over in his hands and he resolved himself to the fact that this was happening, and he could not stop it. They had lived in the shadows much too long.

Now, at age thirty-eight, he despised *the pack* for the long-afflicted abuse he had suffered at their hands. Twenty-five years later and it was time, he thought, as he stared at the seven words on the page.

What would this decision do to his son? For he too was a homosexual, and was beginning the teen years, which could be the toughest on a boy who was completely "out of the closet." The big man put his head on his desk as sobs racked his body. He let them come in waves of misery. Racking his body over and over. Yes, it must be done. They must pay for their crime because no amount of suffering on the inside would make it right. They must confess and the justice system must judge them. It was the only way out of the nightmare—the only way.

Chapter Twelve
The "happer" Days Have Come and Gone
Present Day

The Happer twins had seen better days. They were working long hours at the Preston Power and Electric Company. The downfall of the economy had hit River's Edge hard. Their meager wages had forced them to move in with their father, who still presided as Reverend of River's Edge Baptist Church. Their mother had passed away five years ago.

The house was what John called a Holly Roller Pigsty. Mismatched furniture that had sat in every room of the house. Religious symbols adorned the walls, which made it all the more depressing for the twins.

Paul Happer was kinder than John. He had a son who lived with his mother on the other side of town. Although he and Linda had only dated for a short amount of time, Paul loved the boy deeply even though he had never been a good father. Ryan was his greatest accomplishment—his only accomplishment.

Ryan would soon be a teenager. Paul was feeling the years slip away from him faster and faster. His pledge to spend more time with the boy continued to be a pipe dream. They had both known that for a long time.

John had always been the dominant twin. Even when they weren't living with their father, the Happer brothers had always lived together. They didn't function well alone.Neither of the twins believed in God. They had decided that a *long* time ago. Their father, Reverend Thomas Happer, catered to all the "pretenders" in the town.

Reverend Happer still held out hope that his sons would *find God*. But both men knew that would never happen. Being a Christian was nonsense, and the bigger the Christian the bigger the idiot. Needless to say, they both thought their father was the biggest idiot of all.

Sitting on the brown sagging sofa, John and Paul were probably the most scared they had ever been in their thirty-eight years. *This is the beginning of your end.* God was about to show the Happer twins the price for not believing.

Chapter Thirteen

Last But Not Least

Present Day

Tabitha Preston was getting a divorce. She was leaving Ernie Johnson and finding a life of her own. Why in the hell had she married him in the first place?

Ernie didn't know that Tabitha was planning to leave. She had booked a flight to Los Angeles for her and the boys. Tabitha wanted to be free. Free of her husband, free of her name, and free of the Godforsaken town that had ruined her life. Of course, deep down she knew it was her own decisions that had ruined her life. But, she wasn't going to let those decisions ruin the lives of her sons as well.

Ernie Jr. was already too much like his father. He was a bully. Tabitha was hoping it wouldn't be too late for Ernie to turn that behavior around.

Brian Caster, the local attorney, had the papers drawn up and ready for Ernie Sr. to sign. That had cost her a pretty penny, but it was worth every dime.

She was giving Ernie seventy-five percent of her inheritance. Her twenty-five percent would be invested in lucrative stocks. Besides, Tabitha didn't care about the money anymore. She and the boys would do just fine. Better than fine! They would thrive in a new place, a new beginning for all of them, minus one Ernie Johnson Sr. No father was better than an abusive one. She owed that to her children, didn't she?

Tabitha pulled into the garage. The thunderstorm was now in full swing. Ice was pelting on the windows in a desperate attempt to crack them open.

Ernie Sr. was waiting for her in the kitchen. He was sitting at the table with a look of pure hatred on his chiseled face. For a moment she thought he'd found out about the divorce. A minute later she wished that was *all* it was.

The world crashed in around her when she opened the envelope with her name printed neatly on the outside. Her sobs filled the air, but her husband did not comfort her. He simply walked out of the kitchen, leaving her in torment. There was no one who could save Tabitha Preston. She had doomed herself to a life of hell. Her children would reap what she had sewn, although Tabitha did not realize the extent to which they were all going to suffer.

Chapter Fourteen
The Pain of the Past
Present Day

He drove down the road without realizing that the storm was rising to a fever pitch. He seemed to be looking at the road ahead, but his eyes were very far away. Suddenly, he realized he had stopped in front of the hanging tree. That was what everyone called it, anyway. Every time he saw that tree it almost sent him over the edge. He could not believe that the town council had not voted to have that monstrous reminder of such a horrible crime cut down.

His hands were gripping the steering wheel so tightly his knuckles were turning white and his face was red from the anger pulsating through his body. He thought about the plan that would be carried out very soon.

The chamber rooms would hold four guests. Guests that could be locked up tight and no screams could be heard outside of the chamber walls. The accommodations had taken years to prepare.

Ice was pelting the windows of his car as he drove through the streets of River's Edge. Smiling to himself about the looks on their faces when they had opened those envelopes. Now he would let them think about those words. They had five days to wait. Five long days.

Part Two
The Game

CHAPTER FIFTEEN
THE WAITING IS THE HARDEST PART
PRESENT DAY

Tabitha Preston sat at her makeup table, staring into the shiny glass. She seemed to have aged twenty years in the last five days. Waiting for the bomb to drop had been agony.

Ernie Sr. had spent most of the last five days either drunk or at work. He wouldn't talk about the seven words that had struck their hearts like a dagger. Every time she had tried to bring it up he'd tell her to shut her mouth. If she didn't, he would tell her more harshly. At one point he had raised his hand to slap her across the face.

So, Tabitha finally did shut up. She endured the torment alone. There was no one to talk to about those words or what they meant.

The pack had vowed to never speak again about that Halloween night. Because they knew it would be certain death. Suicide was what Ernie called it when one of them wanted to go to the police.

"You're committing suicide, you stupid piece of shit!" he had yelled. "This is not about you. It's about US. We've made a promise, and by hell you are going to keep that promise."

Then Ernie had pulled out a knife and *the pack* knew he meant business with a capital "B."

"This is what will be waiting for you if you breathe one word to anyone,"

Ernie had said with venom in his voice. Then he whispered, "I'll cut your throat from ear to ear, you fuckin' toady."

The toady believed him. His eyes were wide with fear as he fell on the ground trying to catch his breath. The asthma attack was a bad one. He fumbled for his inhaler, which Ernie kicked out of his hands.

"We are in this together, bitches. Just one big happy fuckin' family," Ernie said as he pointed the blade of the knife at every member of *the pack*. "If any of you dare to tell another living soul, it will be the beginning of your end. You got that, the beginning of the fuckin' end!"

Then he shoved the knife in the back of his pants. He bent over and picked up the toady's inhaler and threw it at his face.

Tabitha shuddered at the memory...*the beginning of the end*.

The most powerful reason none of *the pack* never went to confess was because they did not want to go to prison. Because that was where they would be headed for the rest of their lives!

Another reason they kept quiet was because they were scared shitless of Ernie. Believed he would carry out his threat if any one of them talked. So, they concealed what they had done. Never thinking that after so long a time that it would come back to haunt them. *Oh, how wrong they were*.

Chapter Sixteen
The Price
Present Day

Ernie Sr. was sure the words had to do with money. He'd waited for five days, checking the mail at all hours thinking about how much money the bastard wanted to keep his mouth shut. If he found out who was behind this, he would kill him on the spot. He had no idea who *The Reaper* was, but with his goons out there he believed he would get to this man before the police did—of that he was absolutely certain.

Those were Ernie's thoughts *until* he saw the Happer twins looking his way at work. He was sitting at his desk overlooking the men and women working on the floor below. Suddenly, he could feel someone's eyes. And, when he searched the room he found both of them looking at him, he knew it had nothing to do with money. They were poor as dirt.

Ernie Sr. grabbed his suit jacket off of the chair and made his way down the stairs. The Happers waited for him in the smoky longue. When he walked in he closed the door behind him.

"I think we need to talk, Ernie," said John.

"You received one, too?" Ernie asked.

Paul nodded his head. "So did Vera Tate. We ate lunch yesterday at *Bob's Burger Palace*."

"Sheriff White?"

John nodded.

"What about Todd?" Ernie asked as his blood began to run cold.

"Came in the mail on the twenty-first," Paul said. "What about Tabitha, did she get one, too?"

Ernie stared at the Happer twins, and they knew the answer was yes.

They regarded each other, not knowing what was truly coming for them.

Chapter Seventeen

Like Moths to a Flame

Present Day

They came to him like moths to a flame. He'd thrown a little intrigue and mystery their way and they had eaten it up. He watched them through the window and smiled behind his black hood. How appropriate that he had chosen the *Grim Reaper* for the game to be carried out in the days ahead.

All of them now huddled together on the doorstep, following his directions to the letter. Their instructions were to wait until all four of the invited guests were present before ringing the doorbell.

Now they stood on the porch steps of *the house on the hill*. The house had been deserted for a long time. It was rumored to be haunted, which only added to the excitement of the visitors waiting to enter.

The doorbell rang. *Death* opened the door and extended his arm into the black gloom of the house.

"Welcome," he said and closed the door behind them.

Orange and yellow lights were everywhere in the room. Vampires hung from the ceiling, along with other monsters. Yellow streamers cascaded from the ceiling.

There was a haunting melody playing throughout the house, and as they traveled from room to room the eerie tune got spookier. They kept stepping on triggers and each time a fake creature would jump out and scare them. It was amazing, and just to think they *were* the first ones to go through this haunted house.

Then the Grim Reaper showed them to a door that led down the stairs into the basement. It was dark and menacing.

The Reaper whispered, "This is the best part. Enter if you dare."

And he opened the door and extended his hand toward the stairs.

Chapter Eighteen
Delusions of Grandeur
Present Day

When Ernie Sr. shared the news that *the pack* had all received the same seven words, Tabitha broke into hysterical sobs that made Ernie so mad he did slap her. Right across the face, hard. The powerful whack reduced her to a quiet whimpering.

He needed to *think* and he couldn't do that with Tabitha blubbering all over the place like a blasted weakling. Pacing the floor, he still believed he could control this situation. Find the son of bitch who had left the envelopes and kill him. Hadn't they gotten away with murder once before? They could do it again.

"We're all going to meet at the sheriff's office at nine o'clock this evening," Ernie spat at his good-for-nothing wife. All she had been was an anchor tied to his foot for as long as he could remember.

Tabitha's face went ashen. *The pack* hadn't been in the same room with each other for over twenty years. They couldn't stand the sight of each other because of the memories it invoked. They had been avoiding each other as much as possible in the small town, briefly nodding across the room at church, school functions, or community events.

To be in the same room with the entire *pack* after all these years turned her stomach to mush, and she ran into the bathroom and emptied the contents of the day into the toilet. She wretched and gagged until there was nothing left. Then she put her head against the cool porcelain as the tears streamed down her face.

Ernie Sr. walked into the bathroom and looked at his wife with disgust. "Pull yourself together, you stupid bitch. Get up, get dressed, and put your makeup on like you've done every day of your life for the last twenty-five years. Don't pretend that you finally have a conscience, because we both know better than that, my dear."

When Ernie Sr. walked out of the bathroom, she was more convinced than ever that her husband was completely crazy. He thought that nothing could touch him. He believed that he was in control when everything was so obviously spinning out of their hands like a cyclone.

Tabitha was just about to wash her face and apply a fresh coat of makeup when the phone rang. She heard Ernie Sr. answer the ring. A few minutes later she heard something shatter.

When she ran into the kitchen she saw that the phone had been ripped out of the wall. Ernie had thrown it out of the window, and he now stood with his hands clutching each side of the black porcelain countertop as he tried to quell the rage pulsating through his body.

Chapter Nineteen
Taken
Present Day

Walking into the creepy old house was thrilling for Ernie Jr. He loved Halloween. Loved the true outlandish horror of it all, and when Death had answered the door he thought it was the perfect touch.

The *Grim Reaper* had given them the tour through the house and it was amazing! Finally he led them down to the basement for the end of the tour.

Ryan Happer grinned to himself. This was the coolest haunted house he'd ever seen in his life. Heart thudding, he followed the group down the stairs. Katie Barker glanced back at him and he realized she was really scared.

He patted her shoulder. "Remember, it's not real," he said.

"It doesn't feel right, Ryan," she replied.

"Haunted houses are supposed to feel creepy," he said.

Jake White whistled. "This is so cool. And, we're the first ones to see it! Awesome!"

Ernie Jr. mimicked Jake. "It's so cool. Could you be any more of a dork?" Although Ernie *did think* it was really awesome, until he walked into the chamber and the door locked behind him.

Chapter Twenty
Terror
Present Day

Katie Barker
Katie was weeping quietly as she sat on the bed of the room in which she had been locked. *The Reaper* told them to each choose one of the four rooms and walk inside, just past the threshold of the door. Opening her eyes wide against the darkness she tried to see what was inside the room she had chosen, and then a mechanical door shut behind her, locking her inside. Her heart was thudding and sweat had broken out all over her body. Why hadn't she run away? She knew something wasn't right from the minute she stepped into the house.

She pounded on the door for over five minutes and then cried uncontrollably, finally collapsed into a heap on the floor. What was happening?

The room was furnished with a bed, a chair, a lamp, a small chest of drawers, and four bookshelves, along with hundreds of books. The chest of drawers held six changes of clothes, six changes of underwear, and six pairs of socks. There was an adjoining room with a sink, toilet, and a shower.

Katie had also looked through the books and found that there were many of the classics like *The Picture of Dorian Gray* and poems by Emily Dickenson, books by Steven King and Edgar Allen Poe. So many others she had never read as of yet. She loved to read. Her mom and dad encouraged her reading and bought her as many books as her room could hold.

"Oh, Mom and Dad, please help me," she whispered.

Ryan Happer

What was going on? Ryan thought to himself as he paced around in the small room. The Grim Reaper had locked him in a room in the basement! And, he'd let him? My God, they were stupid to come here. Stupid. Stupid. Stupid.

They had been so excited when they received the cards in their school lockers. It was thrilling to know that only four students had been chosen as the first ones to tour the haunted house. What made it better were the stories that went around about *the house on the hill*. It made it scarier. He'd heard tales all his life about this house. How a little girl had been murdered and her mother had gone insane. Supposedly, her mother had committed suicide in this house. Her ghost reportedly roamed the halls looking for her daughter, never at rest.

But, it was no ghost that had locked him in this room. It was flesh and blood, and by the looks of the place the Grim Reaper was planning on keeping them here for quite a while.

Jake White

Jake knew as soon as he heard the lock click into place that he was in the biggest trouble of his life. He didn't scream or cry or pound on the walls of the door. That would do no good. He was trapped just like the rest of them in the *house on the hill*.

As he sat on the bed staring at the books that lined the shelves, he thought about the stories that he had heard about this old house. A family named Singer had once lived here. After their daughter's murder the mother had committed suicide. Mr. Singer had moved away. The house was placed on the market, but no one would buy a place they thought might be haunted.

But Jake knew better than to believe in ghosts. It was the living that did the damage, not the dead. The living could kill, torture, and bully. He snorted under his breath. Ernie Jr. was evidence of that. He wondered how Ernie was holding up.

Ernie Jr.

Ernie Jr. was losing his mind. He'd yelled and screamed profanities behind the door of the locked room.

The Reaper smiled to himself. Although he had long removed the mask, he still believed that he was Death personified.

Soon he would tell them why he had brought them here. They would know who it was that held the choice of their fate. He sat back in the leather chair and drank greedily from a glass of vodka, the one glass that he had allowed himself in many years.

"Scream all you want, little Ernie," he snarled.

And little Ernie was screaming. The words streaming from his mouth were a testament to the use of bad language that he used all the time. Funny, the ones who seem the strongest usually turn out to be the weakest.

Chapter Twenty-one

Shock

Present Day

Ernie and Tabitha

"What's the matter with you? Have you completely lost your mind? What are the neighbors going to think when they see that broken window?" Tabitha paused for a moment, and when her husband gave no response she said, "Who was that on the phone?"

Still, no response. Her heart began to race like a freight train.

"For God's sake, tell me what's wrong!" Tabitha stood on the other side of the counter, her eyes wide with fear. He raised his golden eyes toward Tabitha and said in a dead voice, "Ernie's been taken."

"Taken? What do you mean, he's been taken? What in the hell are you talking about, Ernie?"

The words exploded out of her mouth, and then she ran to her oldest son's room. She looked around wildly.

Evan appeared at the doorway. "What's the matter, Mom?" he asked. "Why are you crying?"

Tabitha grabbed him by the shoulders and shook him hard. "Your brother, where is your brother?"

Evan began to cry, too. "I don't know, Mom. I don't know."

She hugged Evan close to her and whispered, "It's all right, baby, it's all right."

That was a lie. Tabitha knew with ever-growing certainty that nothing would ever be right again.

Ernie Sr. told Evan to go to his room. A dark thought came to his mind; if only Evan had been taken, not Ernie. It was a hideous, monstrous thought. But it wasn't a surprising thought, because Ernie Johnson had *always* been a *monster*.

Chapter Twenty-two

Together Again
Present Day

Sheriff White sat at the head of the elongated table with the other members of *the pack* around him. His head was pounding. He was telling *the pack* about the phone call he had received. "When the call came in, I wasn't home. The message was left on my answering machine. It was apparent that the caller was using a voice modifier and we now know a throwaway phone that was untraceable. He put Jake on the phone for a moment. Then he took the phone back. He said I would have to choose between my son's life and his death. He called himself *The Reaper*."

Every member of *the pack* had received the same phone call, and Ernie Sr. was about to boil over while listening to what Sheriff White was saying.

The seven sat together in the conference room of the River's Edge Police Office, discussing what their next move might entail. Together again, just like old times. But, they weren't *the shit* anymore. The days when *the pack* ruled the small universe of River's Edge were long gone. That was a certainty; the guillotine was coming down on their heads heavy and sharp. There would be no staving it off this time around. It was the *beginning of the end* for *the pack*.

Todd Barker's voice brought Ray back to the present. "What are we going to do?" he asked. His grief was palpable. His wife, Amy, was waiting in the front office during this private session with *the pack*, and she was a mess.

"I tell you what we're going to do. We are going to find this son of a bitch. I know people in this town that are already looking. People that have ways of finding out the truth. He'll wish he had never been born when I get finished with him," Ernie said through his clenched teeth.

"Ernie, what are you talking about?" Paul Happer shouted, slamming his hand down on the table. "Our children have been taken. TAKEN."

"Who knows what is happening to them this very minute. Katie must be so scared," Todd said to no one in particular.

Ernie shouted back, "I know they've been taken, but I seem to be the only one who wants to find the bastard and make him pay!"

"We're not in control anymore, Ernie," Ray said. "The CISVU is coming in from Washington. They will be our best chance at finding them."

"You better *get* control, Sheriff White," Ernie said and glared at him.

"I'm not thirteen anymore, Ernie. The only thing I care about is getting my son back alive."

Vera Tate hadn't spoken a word since she had arrived. Her voice was barely audible. "We're going to be punished."

"Shut up, you stupid bitch!" Ernie shouted.

Ernie glared at Vera like he was about to throw her across the room.

"This 'reaper,' he knows, but how does he know? Unless, of course, it's one of us?" said John as he looked slowly around the room that had once been called "*the shit.*"

"One of us!" Ernie shouted. "What the hell are you talking about, you son of a bitch? Speak up, John, and tell me where that conclusion came from!"

John stared Ernie down across the table. It was obvious that Ernie's rage was taking over and he could barely contain the fury. He lunged his body toward John. Punches were thrown before Paul and Sheriff White could pull them off of each other. Todd Barker was about to lose his mind; he didn't even realize a fight had just taken place right beside him.

Once Ernie and John had calmed down enough, just enough to talk, silence filled the air around them.

Ernie broke the silence. "John, do you know anything you are not telling us about our children that you would like to share? Because I would like to know where that accusation came from, and I want to know now!"

"It wasn't an accusation, Ernie. Has that thought not gone through your mind? I mean, there were seven of us that heard those words that were placed in the middle of that paper. Please don't tell me that for a split second you haven't contemplated it might be one of us. The only thing I did was bring it out into the open. But, we have no way of really knowing, because if someone in this room has orchestrated this whole plan down to the letter, there is no way they are ever going to put the cards on the table. They have the advantage to win this game, and this time we are flying blind."

John continued to stare Ernie down. It was about ready to reach an all-time high again because they were all losing control.

"What I meant, Ernie," John sat forward in his chair, "is that we are the only ones who know about that night. And, the phrasing on the paper that was given to everyone that clearly states: *This is the beginning of your end.* How would anyone else know that?"

Silence filled the room along with a profound darkness. An all-possessing darkness that *the pack* had never felt before.

Chapter Twenty-three
The Choice
Present Day

Katie Barker
The Reaper had slipped into her room and asked her to call her parents. He had written down what he wanted her to say. Katie did exactly as he asked. Her dad had answered. She read the sentence written on the paper, then *The Reaper* took the phone and told her dad he had a choice—a choice between her life and her death.

The phone call had been made a few hours ago. Katie believed that Ryan, Jake, and Ernie Jr. had been asked to make the same call.

Suddenly, *The Reaper*'s voice came over the loudspeaker at the top of the room. She hadn't noticed the speaker until now. As she listened to his voice, Katie thought that he sounded frighteningly sane. That made her more afraid than ever. A sane person wouldn't make mistakes. A sane person knew exactly what they were doing. A sane person could not be tricked. She listened hard to what *The Reaper* had to say:

"All of you are thirteen or very close to turning thirteen, so I know you will understand what I am about to tell you. While you are guests here, you will be served three meals a day. You will have six changes of clothes.

I suggest you spend your time reading. Expand your mind. Read about the characters that chose light. And also, read about the characters who chose darkness. What made them different and why did they make that decision instead?

Now please, listen carefully to what I have to say. Your parents have a decision to make. They will get a letter that has two choices. Once they receive their final instructions, they will have twenty-four hours to make that decision before twelve midnight on October 31st. Your life is in their hands as the life of another child was in their hands twenty-five years ago. Let us hope, for your sake, they make a better choice this time."

Chapter Twenty-four
Panic
Present Day

Before *the pack* met at the sheriff's office, each home that had received the call had dissolved into panic. They had called 911 and the sirens could be heard all over River's Edge. People came to their windows and walked out on their porches and to the end of the driveway to see the show.

And, it was a show. Word soon spread that four children had been kidnapped. Fear swept through the town like a whirlwind. Rumors ran ramped and knocked heels with each other. Tongues wagged with excitement. The story was probably going to make national news, and the folks of River's Edge were ready and waiting to speak to the reporters about the horrible atrocity that was happening right in their own backyards.

That was exactly what Bobby Cain said to the reporter from CBS: "It's scary. This mad-man is right in our backyards."

Dorthea Bonner was crying when she said, "I just keep thinking, what if it was my daughter? I don't know how those parents are still in their right minds."

"Our hearts go out to the families," Brian Hermann said into the camera.

Neighbors brought food to each family. More than they could have eaten in a week. Fried chicken, ham, mashed potatoes, cakes, pies, and countless other food items that sat uneaten in each kitchen.

Officers held vigil at each house waiting for *The Reaper* to contact the parents with his demands. They had searched each home in the hope of some clue as to who might have taken the children. Confiscating the computers to try and find out if the kidnapper might have contacted them through the internet or email before he had taken them. Phones were tapped, and shifts were set up so that the River's Edge Police Force would be at each house every minute of the day for when and if *The Reaper* made contact again.

Chapter Twenty-five
The Criminal Investigation Team for Special Victims Unit
Present Day

The River's Edge Police Station started to get phone calls about all the missing children at the same time. Police officers had raced to each house to wait for any other calls that might come in so they could glean information on the man and why he called himself *The Reaper*, or to deal with any ransom demands the man might ask for to bring all of the hostage's home safely. Sheriff White had been out on a call but came straight to the police office when he heard what was happening. When he got there and checked his home phone, he found the same message had been left on his answering machine about his son, Jake.

His men had raced to each home where a call had come in about a kidnapping. Thank God his deputy, Bill Martin, had taken over.

He'd dropped into his chair with his head in his hands. When Brian Caster walked into his office he knew he needed a miracle; Brian Caster was the prosecuting attorney for River's Edge. He was tough and had won every case he'd ever prosecuted. Ray had known Brian all his life.

Brian sat down across from Ray's desk. "Ray, I am so sorry that this is happening to you and your son. And, with your son being one of the four that have been taken, it will be hard for you to lead this investigation."

Ray sat back in his chair and looked at Brian.

"You're a great sheriff, Ray. A great leader of this town. But, I can already see the shock and the stress this in putting on you. And, you know a Federal team will most likely be coming in on this."

Ray nodded and closed his eyes.

"You need a man on your team you can trust. You need someone that will go after this lunatic and find those children."

Brian paused for only a moment as Sheriff White raised his sagging head.

"Let me call Reese. He knows the town and the people. You know that he is now the lead of the CISVU in Washington. Let me try and get him and his team here first."

Sheriff White nodded again. He knew a special team would be coming in because so many children were taken at one time. He would rather have someone he knew leading this case. Besides, Reese knew the town inside and out. He'd grown up in River's Edge as well. And, he was good. If anyone could root out the kidnapper and find the kids, it would be Reese. He was their best shot.

"Call him," Ray said.

Chapter Twenty-six

No Sweepstakes in Prison

Present Day

Vera Tate was the first of *the pack* to realize she was going to prison. Maybe because she didn't have a child in the clutches of *The Reaper* she was able to step back and think about it more logically than the others.

They were going to be punished but it wasn't going to be through the death of their children; it was going to be through the legal system. She didn't believe for one minute that The Reaper would really kill four children. If *The Reaper* was trying to get revenge for the murder of Madeline Singer, the last thing he would do was murder four thirteen-year-olds. But, Vera didn't have a voice in this game. She didn't have a child. She didn't have anything except the *Publishers Clearing House Sweepstakes.*

She'd chosen to hurt Madeline because she had everything she didn't. A loving mother and father, exquisite beauty, and she lived in the *house on the hill.* The house had looked down on Vera and reminded her every day that she had been born to a life of misery.

A true evil had come over her that night, twenty-five years ago. The hate flying through her body like a shockwave was so intense that she had lost all control of herself. When she'd come to her senses, it was too late.

As Vera pulled into her driveway after meeting with *the pack*, she knew she was coming back to hell. The only thing that would be different about going to prison was that Vera was pretty sure the *Publishers Clearing House Sweepstakes* wouldn't be delivered in prison. And, everyone knew, *if you don't enter you can't win.*

Chapter Twenty-seven
The Call to an Old Friend
Present Day

When Reese Stone answered the phone, he was in his office going over case files. "Reese Stone," he said as he picked up the call on the first ring.

Brian Caster's voice was on the other line. "How are you doing in Washington, Reese?"

Reese leaned back in his chair. "Sounds like a bit better than you are having at River's Edge."

"Any big cases you working on right now? Would you consider coming home to help us find who has taken these four kids?"

Reese paused and then said, "I am sure the whole town is in shock, especially with all the publicity this case is going to get. If the reporters haven't already started swooping down, it will be sooner than later." He'd seen the news and had been expecting the call. "And, Sheriff White's son is one of the missing?"

"Yes, I don't think he is in any shape to lead the investigation. I asked if we could bring you in as the lead. I wanted to call your team in before they bring in another one. You grew up here. You know the people and the town."

"I'll get the team together. We'll be there in the morning," he replied.

"Thank you. I know it's a lot to process. See you soon."

Reese hung up the phone. My God, he was headed back to River's Edge.

He closed his eyes thinking about his childhood. Many happy times, but along with one nightmare that had never left his heart or mind as he had grown to be the man he was now. How he could never forget Madeline.

Chapter Twenty-eight
Madeline
Present Day

After Reese hung up the phone he walked to the window. Across the street a group of children were playing in the park. Their laughter could be heard through the open glass. It ignited his most powerful memory of Madeline; the melody played in his mind and he drifted back....

"Now, I'm going to serve the tea and cookies. You must wait until the hostess has served the refreshments before partaking of the lovely brunch."

Reese, Brian, and Ray were again listening to words they had never heard before, as usual. They had been invited to the "lovely tea" by a handwritten invitation that asked them to dress for the occasion. All three of them had worn a suit and tie. Brian's suit was almost like new because he had attended his cousin's wedding in Baltimore, Maryland, that past summer; Reese's was shabbier. His mom had bought it at the Goodwill to wear for his baptism last year. Ray White's suit was brand-spanking new and he'd combed his brown hair over to one side and slicked back with some type of hair gel. His brown eyes were wide with appreciation of the display of what Madeline called fine dining.

When they had arrived at her house, she had told them all they looked splendid. She beamed at them from the other side of the door, then stepped aside and said, "Welcome."

Even at eleven years old, Madeline was already a beauty. She had dressed in a pink lace dress with a pink satin ribbon in her hair. Her blonde hair was braided and she looked very grown up. As she poured the tea, Madeline sang the little tune that she often sang when she and the other girls were swinging.

"Cee-Cee, my playmate, come out and play with me. And, bring your dollies three. Climb up my apple tree, slide down my rainbow, into my cellar door, and we'll be jolly friends forevermore."

Reese turned and walked toward his desk, running his hand through his jet-black hair. He reached in his back pocket and pulled out his wallet. He withdrew an old piece of paper that was creased and beginning to fade. Although it was twenty-five years old to him, it was as precious as the day their teacher Mrs. Park had given it to him.

The year before Madeline had died, Mrs. Park had given them an assignment for Veteran's Day. She asked them to create either a poem or poster to show appreciation to those who had given service to our country.

Madeline had seen a news story on television about a man who had served in the Army and had saved the other men in his platoon. But in doing so, he had become paralyzed from the waist down. She had watched as the little boy dropped the sign he was holding and ran to hug his father and then moved around to push his wheelchair.

Reese placed the paper on his desk and began to read the poem Madeline had written for the project as he had done so many times:

Coming Home

He held his mom's hand tightly
In the middle of the crowd.
His little face was beaming
As he looked all around

Banners were flying high
As far as he could see.
Family and friends had gathered
With pride and dignity

There would be a party
Like none they had ever known
And soon he would see him
His daddy was coming home.

Coming home, coming home
A soldier is coming home
Through the fight, he was brave
Many lives had been saved

Let our flag proudly wave
A soldier is coming home today.

A sign he holds in the air
So that all the world will know.
Letters colored big and bright,
"MY DADDY IS A HERO."

A car pulls into the crowd
And the door opens wide
He runs into his daddy's arms
While his mommy cries.

He helps with the wheelchair
To prove that he had grown.
He wants to be just like the man
Who has finally come home!

Coming home, coming home
A soldier is coming home.
Through the fight, he was brave
Many lives had been saved.
A hero is coming home today.

Mrs. Park had entered the poem in a poetry contest and Madeline had won first place. He could see her in his mind with the blue ribbon pinned on her shirt. She'd worn it all day and Mrs. Park had taken her picture for the yearbook holding up a typed copy of the poem. It was wonderful watching her smiling from ear to ear. She was so beautiful inside and out. Madeline was the kind of person who was nice to everyone. It was hard to believe that in less a year she would be dead.

After the murder, Reese asked Mrs. Park if she would give him a copy of Madeline's poem and she gave him one. He felt as though it gave him a part of her spirit, and he'd kept it all these years. Reese folded the poem and placed it back in his wallet, then he grabbed the phone and called the team that would be going to River's Edge, Kentucky, with him. Although he hadn't stepped foot in River's Edge for twenty years, the memories of Madeline burned in his mind like a raging inferno.

Chapter Twenty-nine
Nothing to do but Read
Present Day

Ernie Jr.
Ernie Jr. had screamed profanities until his throat was hoarse. Then he'd torn the room to pieces. The books lay scattered all over the floor, along with the bedsheets and anything else he could find to throw.

After the frenzy, he had curled up in the corner of the room and sat there, tightly hugging himself while he rocked back and forth, back and forth. He refused to cry any tears, so his golden flecked eyes held no semblance of fear. But he was afraid. Scared to death was more like it; at first his fear had come out in anger, but as the hours wore on his emotions turned to liquid. Liquid that was just waiting to fall down his cheeks. The only thing stopping the onslaught of crying was that he knew his father would be embarrassed for him to cry. He could just hear his father now, talking to him as he sometimes did to Evan. "Stop that right now! I'm not raising no namby-pamby girls here in this house. You are a man, and I mean for you to show it instead of crying at the drop of a hat!" Then his father would fly out of the room before his hands could hit Evan for crying. Ernie Jr. knew his father really wanted to beat the crying out of his little brother but would not take the step to do so. His rage would simply take him away from his smallest son to the other end of the house so he didn't have to listen to Evan cry even harder after being yelled at by their father. Words sometimes did more damage than hitting, Ernie thought.

After *The Reaper* came over the loud speaker, Ernie Jr. finally stopped rocking. He sat with a stony gaze and contemplated the words spoken by the nutcase that was holding them hostage. What in the hell was that speech supposed to mean? That his parents would have to make a choice between his life and his death? Then somewhere in the misty haze of his thoughts anger had given way to weariness and he'd fallen asleep.

When he woke up, his coppery hair was a mess and a breakfast tray had been pushed through the flap at the bottom of the door. Ernie Jr. had made a promise to himself that he would eat nothing that the psycho gave him. Unfortunately, Ernie had made that promise before he was hungry. The smell of the eggs and bacon made his mouth water.

So, Ernie ate the food that he had vowed not to eat. Then he did something that he'd never "chosen" to do in his life; he picked up a book and started to read.

Jake White

Jake hadn't slept all night. When the breakfast tray slid through the door, he'd gone to the flap and tried to talk to *The Reaper*. His dad was good at getting people to talk. So, Jake called out, "What did you mean when you said our parents held the life of another child in their hands? I want to understand."

His dad always said that trying to understand the way other people felt was an important part of being a sheriff. It helped build trust. That was important to his dad, having the trust of the town. Jake thought his dad was a great sheriff. And he was a great dad, too. When Jake had told his dad he was gay, he'd hugged him really tight and told him he loved him, that he would always love him, no matter what.

He couldn't imagine that his dad would do anything to hurt another human being. His dad was generous and kind. The people of the town respected and loved him. When he'd been elected sheriff, he'd won by a landslide.

"Please, I want to understand," Jake begged.

But *The Reaper* remained silent. Jake thought that he had paused for a few moments at the door, then nothing. When he could stand the whirling of his thoughts no more, he wandered over to the bookshelf and picked up the book sitting on top. He opened it and started to read.

Katie Barker

After listening to *The Reaper* foretell their fate, Katie thought about the lack of conviction in his voice. He did not mean what he was saying. But, she couldn't imagine that her father would choose to hurt anyone. He'd taken a vow to "do no harm" when he became a doctor. Katie knew that because he had told her many times that it was a code to live by: *First, do no harm.*

Her hope was to be a doctor someday, just like her parents. She wanted to help others the way she'd seen her mom and dad do her whole life. She loved her dad and was the spitting image of him as well, with her dark hair and blue eyes. That long hair now fell over her eyes as she thought of him.

Whatever the decision they had to make, she knew without a doubt her parents would choose her survival. They loved her more than life itself. That scared Katie a bit. To think that she might lose them forever, because Katie knew if they were asked they would give up their own lives to save her.

Her thoughts were a jumbled mess after spending the night in the room without anyone to talk to. She looked at the books and knew she would find comfort within the pages just as she always had, so she opened a book and started to read.

Ryan Happer

Ryan was praying. He had a strong belief in God and that belief steadied him. The comfort of the Lord's spirit surrounded him, and he drifted away within the prayer and heard his Grandpa Happer's gentle voice: "Let the Lord sustain and keep you, let him know your troubles and sorrows. For he is the Lord Almighty and he will be the strength in your darkest hour."

God's spirit did fill him with strength. The light of God lived and breathed in his soul. He prayed for protection. He prayed *The Reaper* would have mercy in his heart. He prayed for the others that had been taken. He prayed for his dad, his Uncle John, and his grandpa, to be filled with the peace to know that he was still alive. Peace now filled his own heart and it took away the fear of death, and as he opened his eyes they fell upon the *Holy Bible*. He opened the book and started to read. His choice was much different from the other three because he was so close to his grandfather.

Chapter Thirty

Now Entering the Game
Present Day

Reese Stone and his team arrived into a horde of reporters. They were like scavengers in front of the police station, thrusting microphones into the faces of the officers as they came and went, hoping to be the one to catch the latest scoop on a man who called himself *The Reaper*.

Deputy Bill Martin met Reese and his team in the front office and led them to the conference room, where Sheriff Ray White and the other officers from the River's Edge Police Force and surrounding counties were assembled.

Sheriff White shook Reese's hand, introduced him, and gave him the floor. He commanded the attention of the room with his mere presence. His dark brown eyes scanned the room.

"Thank you, Ray. Again, my name is Reese Stone and we are from the Criminal Investigation Special Victims Unit in Washington. These are Federal Agents Alicia Davidson, Mark Daniels, and Tyler Parker. They are part of the team that will be helping with the investigation. We are here to assist you in any way possible. As Sheriff White said, I grew up in River's Edge and I want to find the UNSUB that has gripped this town. We've composed a profile of the kidnapper and Agent Davidson is going to share that information with you."

Alicia Davidson walked to the front of the room. She was the perfect picture of a Federal Agent with a tailored skirt and jacket. Her chocolate-brown hair was pulled back from her face and it matched her cocoa skin perfectly.

Like Reese, Detective Davidson had an air of confidence that permeated the room.

"Thank you, Detective Stone. This kidnapper is intelligent. He is most likely a trusted member of the community, someone that knows the town. His confidence allows him a sense of authority. In his mid-thirties to early forties, he has established himself as a prominent member of society. We believe that he is good looking. His looks having helped him become a cunning and crafty man. One in which no one would ever suspect."

Detective Tyler Parker interjected. "This is something that he may have been planning for a long while. There is no other way he could have abducted four adolescents without someone noticing them being taken."

Detective Davidson said, "We know you've interviewed the citizens of River's Edge. Have they presented any clues that might lead us to the UNSUB?"

Sheriff White spoke up. "We've talked with everyone we can think of as of yet—neighbors, the people of River's Edge, and the surrounding areas as well."

Ray had grown into a tall man who was still a bit pudgy around the middle. However, just by looking at him now, he showed a valor that Reese had never seen on Ray's face. He commanded authority as he addressed his deputies and the team of agents.

"We have no leads on the case as of yet. After so many hours of searching the town, not even a shred of evidence." He looked as if death were on his doorstep. But, Sheriff White was still standing. All six feet four inches of him ready to get his son back no matter what the cost. Just by looking at him now, it was obvious that Ray White wore the uniform like a man with a natural ability to lead.

Deputy Martin spoke up. "How can we be sure he's a member of the community?"

Reese Stone answered, "He knows these families. Although we have no idea what he wants from them, we know they have most likely been targeted for a reason."

Agent Davidson said, "While we wait for him to make contact with the parents, continue to talk with members of the River's Edge Community. Try and find a connection between these families—a reason for choosing these four teenagers in particular. Ask again if they have noticed anything out of place. Anything at all that may help us catch this man and bring them back alive."

The team continued to answer a few more questions, and Reese gave them instructions about how the investigation would proceed.

"Agents Parker and Davidson will remain at the station to look over the evidence you have collected so far. Agent Daniels and I will visit the homes of the parents whose children have been taken. The most important piece of information will be how these families are linked. Thank you for allowing us to help with this crime. Like you, we want to bring justice to the town of River's Edge."

Before he and Agent Daniels left, he stepped over to Sheriff White. "We'll do everything we can to bring your son back alive, Ray."

"Thank you for coming, Reese."

Reese nodded and headed for the parking lot. He and Agent Daniels had a lot of ground to cover in the hours ahead. Walking out of the River's Edge Police Department, his thoughts remained on another little girl who had needed his help so many years ago. After this was over, maybe he'd finally be able to let go of the past.

Chapter Thirty-one
Present Day

Reese and Mark Daniels made their way down Second Street, but Reese slowed his car to a stop. It was such a small town, there were hardly any cars on the streets of River's Edge at any time of day or night.

"Are you okay?" asked Mark. "You look like the Devil just walked over your grave."

Reese shifted in his seat and replied, "When I was thirteen, one of my friends was murdered in this town. She was murdered and hung from that tree."

"Oh, man, boss, I'm sorry." His green eyes clearly showed how much respect he had for the man sitting beside him; ten years his senior was known for his hard work and the team looked to him as a father figure of sorts.

"She lived in the *house on the hill*." Reese pointed to the overgrown house that had once been a beacon of pure brilliance. It was a testament to the evil that had rocked River's Edge. "We had been friends since we were seven years old."

"That the reason you became a cop?" Mark asked.

Reese stared at the house intently. "One of the reasons," he replied. "They never caught the murderer."

"Must be hard to be back in this town again after going through something like that, boss."

Reese nodded as he pulled away from the hanging tree.

For the rest of the drive, Mark was silent. Reese was glad Mark didn't ask him any more questions about the murder. That was why he liked his team so much. They knew when it was time to end a conversation.

He swung the SUV into the Happer's driveway, steeling himself for the interview ahead and centering his mind on the matter at hand. Four young teenagers were missing, and it was his job to bring them home.

Chapter Thirty-two

"Happer" Time

Present Day

John Happer answered the door, shook Reese's hand, and asked both of them to come inside. Walking into the house was like entering a religious shrine. Religious emblems, pictures, and figurines were placed all around the small living room. There were many different kinds of crosses on the walls. Two police officers were set up in the kitchen to monitor any calls from *The Reaper*. Reese and Mark both nodded a hello to the officers on duty.

John noticed they had been looking at his dad's collection. "You know, Dad's always been a believer of the freaky kind," John said as he offered them both a seat.

"I've always admired your dad, John," Reese assured him. "He believes there is good in everyone. That alone makes him a man of great character."

Paul Happer walked into the room. He looked as if he hadn't slept in days. His blue eyes were red and watery, and his once white-blond hair had taken on a dull yellow color. It was matted to his head as if he hadn't showered in a while. He stepped over to shake hands with Reese and Mark before sitting down.

"Good to see you, Reese."

Reese stared into the weary eyes of Paul Happer. Paul stared back. It was taking a toll on him, this man who was once part of a pack who called themselves *the shit*. Somewhere between then and now, the Happer brothers had grown up. They weren't the boys Reese remembered who had stolen from their neighbors, egged houses, and bullied other children. They were men, two sad, lazy men who were crippled by the kidnapping of Paul's son.

"We are going to do everything we can to find your son, Paul. But, we need your help. We're here to ask you a few questions," Reese said.

Paul nodded.

"Sheriff White informed us that you received a phone call from Ryan the 26th of October and he told you he was in trouble. Then the man who calls himself *The Reaper* took the phone and said he would contact you in four days with more information. Is that correct?"

Paul nodded again.

"Approximately what time of day did you receive the call?"

"It was 6:00 P.M. on the nose. I know because Jesus came out of the clock and gave his hourly blessing on the house," he said and pointed to the clock on the mantel.

"Did this man give any indication of what his demands would be for getting Ryan back alive?"

"He said he'd contact us in four days."

"Did he give a reason for abducting your son, Paul?"

Paul shook his head.

"He said nothing about a ransom demand?"

"No! He said he had my son and that he would contact me in four days!" Paul shouted.

"Okay, were there any new friends that Ryan was hanging around with recently? Someone you hadn't seen before?"

"Not that I know of, but you might want to talk with his mother, Linda. She would know more than I do about that."

"We'll drive over and talk to her as well. What about school? Were there differences in his grades? Had Ryan been exhibiting behavior that was out of the ordinary?"

Paul shook his head. "He works hard in school, makes A's and B's. I haven't noticed anything different in his behavior. He's a good kid. Ryan wants to be a minister when he grows up, just like his grandpa."

"Then you've raised a great son," Reese said.

"Can't take much credit for that. Wish I could, but he lives with his mom and spends a lot of time with his grandpa."

"Is there anything else you can think of that might help us in the investigation?" Reese asked.

Paul glanced at John and then shook his head. "I've told you everything I know."

"Could we talk with Reverend Happer, by any chance?" Reese asked.

"He's over at the church. Been there holding prayer vigils for the families of the missing children; wants the community and families to know they have a place to go if they need comfort."

"He's a good man. Always has been," Reese said as he and Detective Daniels got up to leave.

Paul walked them to the door. "Ryan is a good young man as well. Just like his grandpa."

Reese turned toward Paul. "You've already let me know that he's a great kid, Paul. I believe you."

"It's just that I don't want you to think he's like I was at that age. He's not. There isn't one mean bone in his body. Please find him, I'm begging you. Please find my boy."

"Our team is good at what they do; we will leave no stone unturned in this investigation. If you think of anything else that we might need to know, call me right away," Reese said as he handed Paul his card. "My cell phone number is on the back. You can reach me with that number anytime, day or night."

Paul took the card, thanked Reese, and watched the two detectives walk down the driveway. As Reese opened the door of the SUV he thought Paul looked as though he had something else to say. Reese hesitated before getting into the vehicle. His dark brown eyes met Paul's blue ones. Then, Paul dropped his gaze and closed the door.

Chapter Thirty-three
Pulling the Strings
Present Day

The Reaper sat in his car on Second Street and watched as Reese Stone drove through the town. He saw him stop by the tree. Still standing after all these years, growing taller and taller, something that Madeline would never get to do; she was in a grave six feet under the ground in the River's Edge Cemetery.

He'd watched the circus of the media storm that was covering the story of *The Reaper*. He'd watched as neighbors and coworkers brought food to the families whose children had been taken. He'd bet his life that if the people of River's Edge *knew* what *the pack* had done to Madeline Singer they wouldn't be bringing them loaves of bread, sweet potatoes, meatloaf, or casseroles that now covered their kitchen counters.

Watching *the pack* grieve the taking of their children gave him a splendid feeling of satisfaction. At least he was giving them a choice. Madeline's mother and father hadn't had a choice. They'd had to endure the horrific pain of seeing their only daughter hung from the tree now blowing in the autumn wind in front of his windshield.

Reese had moved on down the street toward the Happer house. He knew Reese would be asking them all kinds of questions, the same questions he would be asking all the others.

But, there was no way in hell *the pack* would tell them about the letters they had been given a few days earlier. *The pack* would wait for *The Reaper*'s terms and conditions before they even *considered* sharing anything like that with the police.

He was holding all the cards. Two days had passed since his guests had arrived. It was almost time for his next move.

Chapter Thirty-four

No Deals with the Devil

Present Day

Brian Caster had stopped by Ernie Johnson's house hours before Reese and his team left the sheriff's station to conduct the interviews of each family.

They were sitting in Ernie's extravagant living room while Tabitha had gone to get them drinks.

"Are you sure you don't want anything stronger than tea?" Tabitha asked.

Brian accepted the glass. "Tea's fine. Thank you."

Ernie Sr. didn't even glance at his wife as she placed the glass of bourbon on the table next to his armchair. Tabitha took a seat in another chair across from Brian. The flames from the fireplace cast strange shadows across her face.

"I just wanted to let you both know that Reese and his team have arrived in River's Edge," Brian said as he drank slowly from his glass.

Ernie Sr. turned his attention away from the fire and looked at Brian. "I don't give a shit about Reese Stone. Ray should be handling this situation. It's his damn town. Calling Reese in just proves what a weakling Ray is and always will be. I have no idea how that dumbass became sheriff."

Tabitha said nothing as she gazed over at Brian. She'd always thought he had a beautiful smile. He had grown into such a handsome man. Twinkling light green eyes that matched the tie he was wearing this evening. Close-cut brown hair that was already going a bit gray on each side. Even at thirty-eight, he was sculpted and lean. Tabitha knew because she had taken quite a few peeks at his body when he'd come over for the barbecues and the pool parties Ernie Sr. hosted in the summer. Ernie always invited what he considered to be the "bigwigs" in town.

When Brian had drawn up the divorce papers for her, he had taken special care to make sure she would be well protected. *Protected*. How wonderful that would feel. To have someone who would have shielded her from the pain of the world. She wondered why she hadn't noticed Brian when they were younger.

Tabitha had taken one of the strong nerve pills that Todd Barker had prescribed for her when she started to have bouts of depression in the last several years. Actually, she had taken two and right now she was high as a kite.

"Reese is good, Ernie, the best in his field. He is head of the Special Victims Unit in Washington."

"Ray called him in because he can't take care of his own damn town." Ernie walked over to the fireplace, then turned to Brian. "Promise me when this son of a bitch is found that you'll tear him apart in that courtroom, that you'll send him away for the rest of his life."

Brian nodded. "I will prosecute to the fullest extent of the law."

Ernie turned back toward the fireplace with a nod of his head. Then the lids of his eyes grew into narrow slits as he thought *unless I get to him first*.

Chapter Thirty-five
Song and Dance
Present Day

Reese pulled away from the Happer's house and headed toward the outskirts of town.

"He's not telling us the truth. He knows more than he's willing to share about the abduction of his son. Why?"

"I don't know, but when we find out I'm sure it will give us the connection as to why these particular teenagers have been taken."

"It's obvious this is killing him. What would be keeping him from leveling with us?"

"Let's see if the other families give us the same song and dance. Then we'll meet back up with the team and find out if they've uncovered any new information." Reese let out a long sigh as he swept his hand through his jet-black hair and headed for the home of Dr. Todd Barker.

When Reese and Mark pulled into the driveway, there were several cars parked in front of the house. Todd's parents had arrived from Florida, along with his wife's sisters and their families. An unmarked police car was parked in the driveway as well.

Todd's dad opened the door and he welcomed Reese and Mark with a warmhearted handshake. "We heard you were coming to help find our Katie girl," he said to Reese.

The handshake turned into a hug, which Reese returned. Todd's dad had been his primary care physician until Reese's family had moved away from River's Edge. When he was a little boy, Doc Barker had always remembered his favorite flavored lollipop was lemon. He'd pull one out of his coat pocket at the end of every visit.

Reese had heard that Doc Barker had retired a few years ago and Todd had taken over the business.

Dr. Barker Sr. led them into the living room. Todd and his wife were sitting close together on the leather sofa. Todd stood up when they walked in the room and offered both of them a seat. After all the introductions had been made, Dr. Barker Sr. ushered everyone out of the room so that Reese and Mark could talk to Todd and Amy in private.

Once they were settled and had declined food or drink, Reese began to ask the same questions he'd asked Paul Happer.

Todd said the call had come in around 6:00 P.M. He explained that Katie said she was going to her friend Angela's house for a study session. When the police questioned Angela, she said that they'd had no plans to get together that afternoon.

"Why do you think Katie would lie to you about where she was going?" Reese asked.

"We have no idea." Todd shook his head.

"She's such a good girl," Amy broke in. "She has never lied to us about anything like this before."

"Any changes in behavior over the last few weeks, new friends or activities that might differ from her regular schedule?" Mark asked.

"Her behavior is always outstanding and if she's been hanging around with anyone new, Amy and I don't know. I can't imagine that Katie wouldn't introduce us to a new friend that she might have made. Nothing in her schedule has changed. She has volleyball after school on Tuesdays and Thursdays, student council meetings on Wednesdays. She's the eighth-grade class president. Takes all advanced classes. Says she wants to be a doctor like her old man."

Todd's eyes welled up with tears. He was at a breaking point, and Reese made his move.

"Todd," Reese leaned forward, "do you have any idea why someone would take Katie?"

Todd shook his head no but his body language suggested otherwise. His shoulders slumped over and his head nodded yes to a question that was answered with a "no."

"Any idea at all as to why she was targeted by the kidnapper as one of the four teenagers who have been abducted?"

Todd shook his head and looked down at his lap. He did not make eye contact with Reese or Mark.

"Did *he* give any *indication* as to why he's taken your daughter during the phone conversation last night?"

"He said he would contact us in four days," Todd Barker choked out and looked straight at Reese. "He said we would have to choose between her life and her death!"

As Reese pulled out of the driveway he felt like he was finally getting somewhere with the case. He had pushed Todd a bit further with his questioning because he seemed more anxious, like a bullet ready to explode out of the barrel of a gun.

As they walked back to the SUV, Reese said, "Well, we finally got some information that might help us in this investigation. I am absolutely sure that the other parents were given that decision as well. We didn't get that from the other interviews. But I could tell Told was about to have a nervous breakdown."

"So, this is nothing to do with money, boss?"

When they got back into the SUV, he rubbed his eyes and took some medicine for the headache coming on. "No, not for money. I think this is about revenge. And we have no idea how far this man that calls himself *The Reaper* will go to get what he obviously wants. If he did say a choice between life and death, then we have got to speed up the search in any way possible."

Chapter Thirty-seven
Date with the Devil
Present Day

Ernie Sr. opened the door and glared hard at the two men standing on his doorstep. Unlike the other two families, Ernie did not dispense with formalities. He stood in the doorway like a cobra ready to strike.

"Hello, Reese," Ernie sneered. "Come back to help the poor souls of River's Edge?"

"If by poor souls you mean your children, then yes, I've come to help," Reese replied in a tone that was just as deadly.

"We don't need your help."

"I think you do need my help, Ernie."

Ernie snorted. "You think I give a shit what you think?"

Reese's face hardened while he tried to hold back his temper. "We're here to try and find your son. Or, don't you give a shit what happens to him either?"

Brian Caster reached Ernie just as he lunged at Reese. Grabbing him by the arms, he forced him back into the foyer. "Get a hold of yourself, Ernie. You can't help Ernie Jr. if you end up in jail. And that is exactly where you're going to be if you don't calm down. Is that what you want? To be sitting in a jail cell when the next call comes from the man who has your son?"

Ernie pushed Brian away. Although he did manage to get control of the rage still burning under his skin like a runaway flame. He stormed away from the door just as the officers appeared in the hallway. They had heard the shouts and left their posts by the phone to see what was happening.

Brain assured the two men on duty that everything was fine. He turned to Reese and held out his hand. "It's been a while. Thank you for coming, Reese."

Reese returned the handshake, introduced Brian to Mark Daniels, and they followed Brian into the beautifully decorated house. Expensive pieces of art hung on the walls of the family room. The fireplace crackled as it sparkled off the glass-topped tables.

The devil's lair, thought Reese while his eyes surveyed the room.

Ernie Sr. had taken his usual seat by the fire and didn't look up as the three men entered the room. Tabitha turned her head mechanically in their direction. She smiled a woozy smile and stood up to welcome them. However, a wave of dizziness swam inside her head and she had to sit back down.

"Tabitha, you remember Reese, and this is his partner, Mark Daniels," Brian said.

"Reese," she slurred. "Please come in and have a seat. Can I get either of you something to drink?" She tried to stand up again, but it was useless.

"They won't be staying long enough to have a drink. So sit down before you fall down," Ernie snarled.

Tabitha looked down at her hands, which were shaking like leaves.

"We're fine, Tabitha. Thank you for asking. We're here to talk about Ernie Jr. We'd like to ask some questions that might help bring him home."

Tabitha nodded with a weak smile on her face. Her eyes were bloodshot as though she'd been crying a great deal, and her pupils were dilated so much that the violet of her eyes were barely visible. Although she was falling apart, she still managed to look beautiful. Her chestnut hair fell across her shoulders in chocolate waves.

"We've already told Sheriff White everything we know," Ernie snapped.

"We understand how difficult this must be for you," Mark Daniels replied. "But Sheriff White's son has been taken, too, placing him under a great deal of stress. That impedes his ability to think clearly about this investigation."

"This won't take very long," Reese interjected. "About what time did you receive the phone call from Ernie Jr.?"

Ernie sat stone-faced staring at the fire.

"It was a few minutes after six," Tabitha said in a rushed voice.

"What did Ernie Jr. say, exactly?" Reese asked.

Tabitha glanced at her husband before answering. "He said he was in trouble."

"Was that all?"

Tabitha nodded as she looked down again at her hands clasped tightly in her lap. "Then someone else took the phone and said our son had been taken."

"Do you have any idea why someone would take your son?"

"No, we don't!" Ernie shouted. "We've already answered these fucking questions."

Reese ignored the outburst. "Did the kidnapper allude to the reason your son has been taken?"

"He never alluded to anything except that he had taken our son. And, if you're here to help find him, why aren't you out there looking for him instead of in here giving us the third degree?" Ernie's voice raised another octave.

"Ernie, Reese is trying to make sure he has all the details of the phone conversation so that his team can better understand the situation at hand," Brian explained.

"Did the kidnapper state his terms for returning Ernie Jr. unharmed?" Reese tried again.

"No, he said he would contact us in four days! So that means two days are already gone while we sit here answering questions we've already answered. This is bullshit. Why don't you stop fucking around and look for him instead of wasting the time we have left?" Ernie stood up and stormed out of the room.

Reese looked at Tabitha, whose eyes were now brimming over with tears.

"Tabitha," Reese said softly, "is there anything else you can think of that might help us find your son?"

Tabitha shook her head.

"I'm going to leave you my card. You can reach me anytime with that number. If you think of anything else, please call me."

Tabitha took the card. Then she grasped Reese by the hand. "You will do everything possible to find Ernie Jr.?"

Reese gave Tabitha a reassuring nod of the head. "Yes, we will do our very best to find all of them."

Brian Caster told Tabitha that he would walk them out since he was leaving as well. When they reached the driveway, Mark Daniels let out a long breath. "What an asshole."

Brain laughed sarcastically. "No doubt about that. Ernie Johnson has been an asshole since the day he was born."

The three men talked about the case and discussed why these four teenagers were the ones targeted for the abduction. It had to be for a specific reason that was eluding all of them right now.

"We are positive that the parents are lying. But, why in the world would they need to lie? It is definite that it is killing all of them," said Mark.

"Well, when we find out the reason, I am sure that will bring us much closer to The Reaper." Reese ran his hand across his face.

They went off in different directions. Reese and Mark still had a few people to interview before going back to the station. Glancing in the rearview mirror as they pulled away from the house, Reese thought to himself that the word "asshole" was too good a term to describe a man like Ernie Johnson.

Chapter Thirty-eight
The Best Burger in Town
Present Day

The Reaper sat in the back booth of Bob's Burger Palace, watching Vera Tate. She moved slowly from table to table, taking orders and delivering food to the customers. When she ambled in his direction, he placed the newspaper he was pretending to read on the white tabletop so that he could place his order.

Vera grinned at him with a tilt of her head. Her pink uniform clung tightly to her ever-expanding middle, looking as if the buttons might burst and put someone's eye out at any moment.

"Will you be having the usual?" she asked.

"No, I think I'll have a burger loaded with everything this evening. And, give me two orders of fries. I feel like living dangerously." He gave her a wink.

Vera blushed under the thick makeup that covered her face. Her bright pink blush and blue eyeshadow looked like the frosting on a birthday cake. "I like a man who lives on the edge."

"So that's the type of man you like?" he replied with a look that made her blush even more.

She scribbled his order hastily, her embarrassment showing. Not knowing how to respond, she took his menu quickly and walked away.

He watched her hefty frame walk behind the counter to give his order to the cook. She looked his way and he smiled at her before picking up his newspaper.

The headline of the *River's Edge Post* was about the kidnapping of the four local teenagers. He read the entire story as he waited for his food to be delivered, wondering how his guests were doing, if they were taking the opportunity to expand their minds by reading the books that had been placed in each room. He'd chosen the books very carefully. One story in particular had been marked for their reading pleasure.

Chapter Thirty-nine

Freaked Out

Present Day

Ernie was so scared. But if he did get out, he would never admit that to his father. There was no laptop, no cellphone, no music, no anything that could keep his mind company, and that was the reason that he decided to read the books that were left in his room.

He was reading one of the short stories that had been left on the top of the bookcase. He'd just finished "The Lottery" by Shirley Jackson. It had freaked him out to the point of emptying the contents of his stomach into the toilet.

The story began with the town getting ready for a lottery that was held every year. The people seemed to be excited but apprehensive at the same time. Soon, it became apparent to Ernie Jr. that this was a lottery that no one wanted to win. At the end, the town *stoned* the lady who had been unfortunate enough to get the piece of paper that had a black dot in the center. They'd even given her three-year-old son a rock to throw at her in sacrifice for a good harvest. Her husband hadn't even come to her rescue. He'd participated in the horrible atrocity.

The man had obviously meant for him to read the story because the book was the only one sitting on top of the bookcase. The story had a bookmark placed in front of it with a picture of an angel dressed in white.

Could there possibly be a connection between this story and their parents? The man had said they had held the life of another child in their hands. He'd said he hoped they chose better this time. What the hell did that mean? What in the hell was this lunatic talking about?

Katie Barker

When Katie had picked up the book, she knew that the man had intended for her to read it. She'd leafed through the pages and found the bookmark of the angel in white. The story had caused a lump in her throat that wouldn't go away.

She sat on the bed wishing to God she hadn't read the story. It chilled her to the bone. The picture of the town stoning the woman was burnt into her mind. It was sick—a sick story of a group of people who stoned members of their town every year in the hope of a good harvest. The worst part of the story was that no one felt remorse over killing the woman. They went on with their day to day lives, thankful that they hadn't had the winning lottery ticket.

Katie had looked through all the other books on the shelves. They now sat in piles all around her on the floor of the tiny room. Not one other book contained a bookmark. Out of all the stories he'd chosen for them to read, "The Lottery" was the most important to him. *Why?*

Jake White

Jake had picked up the book in the hope of taking his mind off what The Grim Reaper had said when he came over the speaker. He knew his dad would do anything to save him, but he was in the hands of a freaking madman.

After reading "The Lottery" he stared into space; his stomach twisted with a dread unlike anything he had ever experienced in his short thirteen years. Long ago they had stoned homosexuals for what they considered to be sinful behavior. However, they thought nothing of the murder they were committing. In their minds, they were convinced that the stoning of a human being was not as sinful as being a homosexual. How did that compute in their minds?

And what in the world could this book have to do with their parents? His dad was a good man. The type of man that would give his own life to save his son; he'd jump in front of him to keep him from being stoned to death, unlike the family of the woman that was sacrificed in the story.

It was apparent that some of the people in the little town of New Hope, Maine, where the stoning took place, felt that the killing was wrong, but just like so many stories in history, they were too afraid to take a stand against society. Shirley Jackson made a clear point to the reader that when good people stand by and do nothing to stop the injustice in the world, history will not be changed. If just one person in the crowd had spoken up to stop the stoning, other voices would have joined them. One person could have made the difference in this story if they had possessed the strength to stand up for what was right.

Walking into the little bathroom, he gazed in the mirror that hung above the sink. Looking at his reflection, he saw so much of his dad's face. He was a great deal thinner than his dad, but he had the same chin, nose, and hazel eyes. Those eyes now bore the sadness of despair and loss. Would he ever see his dad again?

Ryan Happer
Ryan had been reading the *Bible* for a long while. It comforted him knowing that God's presence was near. Reading God's word always put hope in his heart. It cleared his mind and calmed his anxiety.

Standing up to stretch his legs, Ryan walked to the bookshelf. He'd noticed the book on top, but the *Bible* had called out to him with such force that he hadn't thought much about why the book was out in the open unlike all the others. Now, as he paged through the short stories his eyes came to rest on an angel in white, bookmarking a story that Ryan had read last year in English class. It was a startling work of fiction and Ryan wondered why in the world the man would want him to read the story of such a brutal murder. What was he trying to tell them? Was this meant to be a clue as to why they had been taken?

Pushing that thought away he returned to the bed and the *Bible*, where he found solace within the pages of the greatest book ever written.

Chapter Forty
The Wages of Sin
Present Day

He watched them from the back pew of the River's Edge Baptist Church. The people with their heads bowed as they asked God for his mercy; they asked for his guidance and love in sending a lifeline to the families in need, to give them strength in this time of deepest despair.

Reverend Happer prayed with them and offered words of comfort to his charges. Even though his grandson had been taken he seemed to stand steadfast in his convictions. The members of the church offered hugs of comfort, but it was obvious he was the one comforting them, with his strong belief in something greater than himself.

Candles burned all around the wood-paneled room. Their yellow flames flickered softly on the face of the reverend, steadfast in his fight against the wages of sin.

How many times had he sat through the teachings of Reverend Happer? As a little boy, he went to church every Sunday. Sitting in the uncomfortable pew, he'd listened intently to the stories from the Old and the New Testament as the kindhearted Reverend taught lessons of repentance and everlasting life.

He'd raised his voice in song with the other members of the church as they praised God within the walls of this room. Too bad that most of them didn't live the lives they pretended to live each Sunday. Maybe if they had, Madeline's family would have found justice for the murder of their only child.

As the people came and went, some of them stopped in polite conversation with him. They expressed their concern over the victims, and tears sprang up in a few of their eyes when talking about what might happen to the four teenagers if they weren't found soon.

But, *The Reaper* didn't have to wonder about what *might happen*. He'd known since he was a child that "the wages of sin is death."

Chapter Forty-one
Beacon of Hope
Present Day

Reese and Mark pulled into the parking lot.

"The picture of a perfect little hometown church," Mark said, looking at Reese. "Is this where the people of River's Edge come to confess their sins?"

"The people of River's Edge don't confess their sins," replied Reese as he got out of the SUV.

Walking through the doors of the church took Reese back again to the murder of his friend. Her funeral was held here, and he'd sat with his mom and dad watching the parade of mourners. Drama filled the church as many people wept for the little girl and her parents. But to Reese, most of the sorrow was a downright lie. The people were just thankful it wasn't them sitting directly in front of the coffin. They were happy to go home to their families, alive and well, shutting their doors with indifference to the heinous crime.

When it was his turn to greet Madeline's parents, they wrapped Reese in their arms and he'd clung to them for dear life as his chest heaved in gut-wrenching sorrow. He cried in their arms for a very long time, her parents allowing the tidal wave of emotion to ebb and flow until it began to subside. As they held him he murmured, "I'm sorry," until the words couldn't find their way to the surface anymore.

Madeline's parents tried to comfort him to no avail. They told him over and over again that it wasn't his fault. But he and Brian had left Madeline by herself that night. If they hadn't raced away from her, if he hadn't wanted to prove what a bigshot he was by outrunning Brian, Madeline would still be alive. They'd left her alone. Oh, God, why had they left her alone?

Reverend Happer's hand on Reese's shoulder brought him out of the painful memory. "God has brought you back to us," Reverend Happer said. Reese noticed that the reverend had lost most of his hair; what hair he had left was completely gray. He'd also put on a few more pounds around the middle. However, his face still held the same look of unequivocal grace that Reese remembered from his youth.

"A less faithful man might say it was the Devil who brought me back," Reese spoke in a quiet voice.

Reverend Happer paused for a moment, then replied just as quietly, "God works in mysterious ways."

"God is a mystery," Reese agreed, staring intently at the grandiose painting of Jesus hanging on the cross that adorned the front of the church. Then he quickly introduced Reverend Happer to Mark Daniels and the three men sat down together.

They talked for a long while about the reverend's grandson. About Ryan's charity work at the hospital, the campaign that he and Jake White had created to raise money for patients with HIV, along with volunteering his time at the nursing home reading to the residents on a regular basis. Paul was right; his son had not followed in his footsteps. Whether nature or nurture had factored into this equation was not evident. What was evident was that *Ryan Happer was a soldier, a soldier of faith.*

The absolute truth hit Reese full throttle and that was when he really looked into the soul of the man sitting before him. Reverend Happer truly believed that God was the one who had brought him back to the town. For the purpose of bringing his grandson back alive. *He* had become the *beacon of hope* that was holding the reverend in one piece.

Chapter Forty-two

The *house on the hill*

Twenty-four Years Ago – Christmas Eve

It stood above the town in the misty winter fog. The pearly, regal frame hovered in the sky like a glimpse of heaven itself. The white twinkling Christmas lights lit up the night for all to see, outlining the magical presence of the *house on the hill*. All the eyes of River's Edge taking in the splendor of the mansion bathed in a breathtaking glow.

Every year the house illuminated the valley from the first of November to the second of January. It could be seen from every vantage point from the streets below and from far down the banks of the Ohio River. To a barge captain it may look like a ship passing in the night on a sea that drifted along at the top of the world.

The annual Christmas party was in full swing by seven P.M. that snowy eve. Full of laughter and spirits, friends and family spread throughout the house filled with soft holiday music, brightly wrapped presents, and a delectable array of delicious food.

Reese, Brian, and Madeline had slipped up the stairs to the tiptop room and were looking at the stars from the magnificent telescope that Madeline's father had purchased the year before. Gazing at the orbital globes that lit up the atmosphere made them feel very small, indeed. But it assured them that beauty was strong within the universe.

Although the planets and stars were a treasure to behold, Reese thought they couldn't hold a candle to Madeline. She was in a class all by herself.

The three friends talked and laughed for hours that evening, the kind of laugh that leaves you breathless, that makes your stomach hurt with the feeling of utter happiness—pure glee!

It was the last Christmas they would spend together. The last time that the luminescence of the lights would cast their captivating spell. Because after that Christmas, the *house on the hill* fell dark.

Below
Another Christmas party was in full swing on that same evening of December 24th. Anthony Preston also threw an extravagant shindig every year. The Preston house sat at the bottom of the valley on the main road, which looped and stretched into Pineville, the next town over.

Unlike the *house on the hill*, it was the most rudely imposing home for many miles north, east, south, or west of the town. The sharp brick red of the house looked like it was bleeding profusely against the white of the snow continuing to fall. This million-dollar monstrosity held all the warmth of a huge stone castle.

The pack sprawled in Tabitha's bedroom smoking a joint. MTV was blaring from the television set that was mounted to the wall. Ernie and Todd were telling dirty jokes, which had them busting a gut throughout the entire evening.

Ernie and Tabitha finally ended up in an empty bedroom where a hot and heavy make-out session had ensued. Doped out of their minds with hormones raging, Tabitha gave in to Ernie's relentless pressure to go all the way.

She'd gone into the bathroom to clean herself up and looked out the window at the glistening snow falling in the multicolored Christmas lights arranged perfectly around the yard. Then, her gaze tilted upward. From below, the *house on the hill* was transfixed in her mind with the unblemished brilliance of an exquisite diamond. It was a cruel reminder of everything she wanted and needed so desperately in her life. She wanted to know what true love felt like, to be cared for in the way that Madeline was up there in the house that looked like a palace. Madeline was so lucky to have both her mother and her father. They went to every school function and helped with all parties as well. And, she also had Reese and Brian at her side at all times. Both such loyal friends. What she wouldn't give to be Madeline Singer for even one day.

Chapter Forty-three

Four

Present Day

He knew the four teenagers now sitting in the chamber rooms were contemplating life as they never had before. They were facing the thought of "spring eternal" being ripped from the tender bloom of youth.

In watching them grow up, he'd realized they weren't the monsters he imagined they would become. They *were not* copies of their parents. Even Ernie Jr. wasn't a true testament to the calculating spawn from hell that was his father. No, Ernie Jr. seemed to be a "normal type" of mean and nasty in comparison to his parents.

This had made his plan much harder to carry out. If the *four* now occupying the space underneath the *house on the hill* had begun to show the *signs* that were prevalent when Madeline was murdered, he'd be feeling no remorse over the terror and pain he was choosing to inflict upon them. But, they were the key to *his* redemption. They may well hold the redemption of the entire town in their young hands. At the very least, they were the ultimate triumph in the long awaited justice for the brutal murder of Madeline.

It was 8:00 P.M. and he'd prepared the third meal of the day for his guests. He knew what would be waiting for him when he pushed the trays underneath the small flap in each door....

Ernie Jr. had stopped using foul language and would say nothing, Jake White would try to engage him in conversation in the hope of understanding "why" he'd been taken, Katie's crying would sting his ears and Ryan Happer would pray loud enough for him to hear in the belief that God would *save them all*. And, maybe by some miracle he would…..

Part Three
Endgame

Chapter Forty-four
Connection
Present Day

Brian Caster sat in front of the camera waiting to be interviewed by Helen Marks herself. As the story of the crime began to make national news, many reporters and talk show hosts were vying for the first shot at an interview with Sheriff Ray White, but because he was in no state for this type of public scrutiny he asked Brain to "deal" with the media circus now taking place in his town.

Alicia Davidson sat to his right. She was Reese's right-hand woman and a no-nonsense, shoot-straight-from-the-hip, special agent extraordinaire. She was ready to field any questions that might jeopardize the investigation. Because Brain had lived his whole life in River's Edge, it would be better for him to make an appeal to *The Reaper*. There was no doubt in the minds of the special agents that the suspect was a local yokel. So, Brian Caster might have the best shot at gaining his attention.

Microphone pinned in place on the lapel of his black suit, Brian waited for Mrs. Marks to direct her attention toward him and his crimson red power tie. He glanced at Alicia, who looked ready to take on a hurricane. Grinning to himself, he was happy to have her seated next to him. He'd seen Helen Marks in action.

Focusing on the TV monitor, he heard that she was now in the process of introducing them to thousands of viewers. The live feed from River's Edge to

New York had been linked through satellite. Helen was coming in loud and clear through his earpiece. He thanked her for the introduction and answered every question about the kidnapping. Then she asked her final question.

"Mr. Caster, is there anything you would like to say specifically to the person responsible for this crime?"

"Yes, Helen," Brian answered as he looked directly into the camera. "The lives of four young teenagers are in your hands. I implore you to make the right decision. Spare the lives of these innocent victims. You have the ability to save them. The choice is yours."

After he got up from the chair and had thanked Alicia, he walked toward the door. Brian turned to say goodbye to Reese but saw that he and Alicia were in deep conversation and they were headed over to the other members of their little group from Washington.

"Hmm...," Brian hummed to himself; maybe they had stumbled upon a clue? Day after day Sheriff White looked as if a small wind could blow him over, and Ernie Sr., well, Ernie Sr. was continuing to lose his mind in a hazy sea of rage.

"The very complexity of this case is that he used a throwaway phone. So we are in the dark on that part of the investigation," stated Alicia.

"Well, we have the statements from all of the parents that *The Reaper* did in fact make those calls and he said the same thing to all of them. They have told us over and over how they spoke to their children at that time as well," Reese said. "So, what you're telling us is that we have *nothing* on *The Reaper* as of right now?"

"No, I am afraid we don't. Like I said before, it seems like we are flying blind." Mark ran his large hands over his face. They were getting nowhere.

"This has just opened another problem," said Alicia with a sigh. "I mean, now *The Reaper* could even be one of the parents, right? Because, we have no hard evidence of the phone that was used. Why in the world would any of these parents put their own child through something like this? I can't believe it would be any of them." Alicia frowned. "They are so distraught."

"Well, it's one more connection in the case," Mark interjected.

Reese closed his eyes and memories flooded his mind from a time far away, twenty-five years ago.

Chapter Forty-five
Contact
Present Day

Sheriff White watched from the door of the Prosecuting Attorney's Office as Brian Caster answered each question Helen Marks threw his way. He was as natural in front of the camera as he was in a courtroom. Ray knew he'd made the correct decision in asking him to handle all publicity the case was attracting.

He hadn't had one wink of sleep in the last twenty-four hours. Last night, along with Reese and his team, they had gone through every interview conducted in the town, reviewed the profile of the UNSUB, and looked at all the evidence they had accumulated in the case, which wasn't much.

So far, the CISVU had only one connection between the four teenagers who'd been kidnapped and that was the same phone call each of them had received. Ray knew it was just a matter of time. Those letters they had gotten from *The Reaper* were just one of another that would be coming their way. His decision to keep the parents out of the spotlight came from the ever presence of knowing how the game was going to end.

Ray unlocked the door then closed it behind him. He walked to his metal desk, footsteps heavy and slow. Swaying slightly, he sat down heavily in his chair. A cold sweat popped out all over his body and his hands shook uncontrollably. His breath became a small wheeze as he tried desperately to get the air into his lungs. This was his second attack today. Pulling his inhaler from his pocket, he sucked the mist deep into his chest as he stared at the letter placed on his desk. He picked it up and began to tap it against his calendar while his mind was full of thoughts of Madeline. To this day, he just could not wrap his mind around the fact that he had done nothing to save her that night. He carried that burden with him every day.

Ray picked up the phone and called every member of *the pack* to see if they had received their letters as well. They decided to meet at Vera's because her house was the only one not under surveillance.

Chapter Forty-six
Here We Go Loopty Loo
Twenty-five Years Ago – All Hallows' Eve

When Reese and Brain had raced away to Front Street, Madeline slowed to take a close look at the Halloween decorations that festooned the eccentric little town. Ghosts and goblins hung from the trees; orange lights blazed from houses outlined in spooky glory. A mummy stood on the porch of one house holding a sign that said: "Brake for candy!"

Another house sported a huge cardboard Dracula that was fastened to the front door. His mouth seeped red blood; fangs protruded and its eyes looked like he'd been hit up side of the head one too many times. She thought he was the perfect picture of a loony-toony vampire who might have drunk the blood of a crazy person.

A song came to mind that matched his eyes perfectly. It was a silly song that her mother sang with her when she was feeling blue, always making her giggle in spite of herself. "This song is for you, loony loopy long teeth!" she said, smiling.

"Here we go loopty loo, here we go loopty lye. Here we go loopty loo, all on a Saturday night." She sang the verse three times as she twirled in her white princess gown. She skipped backward singing the fourth verse, laughing and waving goodbye to the baffled-looking cross-eyed monster.

Turning back around, Madeline came face to face with the real monsters that had been waiting and watching.

CHAPTER FORTY-SEVEN
THRILLER NIGHT
TWENTY-FIVE YEARS AGO – ALL HALLOWS' EVE

While the two zombies waited for Madeline by the banks of the river, they searched through the bags of candy. They traded each other for their favorites. Reese loved Snickers and Brian had a passion for anything fruit flavored. He popped a cherry Life Saver in his mouth.

Sitting on the top of the dirt-laden bank many feet above the water, the boys seemed to fade into the backdrop of the town, their black-and-gray clothing matching River's Edge in perfect harmony.

"If zombies did exist, River's Edge would be their home away from home," Brian said as he tore more of the paper from *the pack* of Life Savers that Reese had traded for the candy bar.

"Zombies don't exist," Reese pointed out.

"I said *if* they existed. Don't you think this town would be the perfect place for a horror movie to be filmed?"

"It would make for good scenery, that's for sure."

"I can't wait to get out of this town. It'd be nice to live somewhere sunny all year 'round."

"Instead of a seventy-percent chance of gray and gloomy. Yeah, I hear ya."

Brian looked around. Where was Madeline? It couldn't be taking her this long to catch up with them.

A car went by with its window down and Brian and Reese heard "Thriller" spilling loudly from the speakers. The lyrics pulsated through the speakers like an omen of death.

Chapter Forty-eight

The Omen
Present Day

Katie Barker

Katie had showered after eating her breakfast that morning. Although there were still six changes of clothes in the drawers, she had only changed her underwear and socks. She still wore the scarlet-and-gray Ohio State jersey and the blue jeans that she had on when they walked into the *house on the hill*. The clothes felt like a link to home. She remembered the day her mother had relented and allowed her to buy the two-hundred-dollar pair of jeans. They were a reward from all of her hard work at school.

Lying on the bed, her eyes focused on the bookmark of the angel in white. The angel wore a crown of gold on her head and seemed to be looking down from heaven above. Her face washed in glorious light, wings arched in flight, suspended in elegance.

Was she in fact meant to be the angel of death? She marked the story of a woman who had been stoned by her friends and family. Looking at the face of the angel, Katie believed she was staring at an omen of deepest proportion. It was obvious that *The Reaper* wanted revenge on their parents from something that happened long ago. He wanted them to read books about good and evil. Was it a lesson on walking in the dark or shining in the light? If that was true, then it was obvious that many years ago her father had made the wrong choice.

What in the world had he done?

The Reaper alluded to the fact that their parents must have chosen a dark path when they were younger. It was very hard to wrap her head around the possibility that her father would ever commit a crime that involved hurting another person. But here she was, being held in the basement of the *house on the hill*. And the man who called himself *The Reaper* was very convincing. She knew that there was a young girl who had been killed in this town a long time ago before she was born. There were stories about this house being haunted. Could this be the link in the chain? She pondered over the situation. Was that the reason they were here? Because of the murder? Could their parents have committed murder? Darkness felt like it was seeping into her heart as she thought more about the angel in white.

Jake White

Jake had tried to talk to *The Reaper* to no avail each time the tray came through his door. He'd asked him different questions, hoping to get any kind of response from his captor.

But, there was never a response. Sometimes he knew *The Reaper* paused before heading away from the door, but Jake was now convinced the man would never engage in any type of conversation. This silence was a testament to the "iron will" of the man who was holding them hostage.

Just like the "iron will" of the town who had stoned the young wife and mother in the hope of a good crop. The people of New Hope, Maine, felt it was their duty to sacrifice the one to save the many. How grotesque this way of thinking was to Jake White. His dad would never, ever sacrifice even one member of his town, let alone one per year. Jake's dad was an "all for one and one for all" type of man.

Wasn't he?

That small omen of doubt made him waver on the brink of desperation.

In his eyes his father was a hero! A true man of justice. He was also a very kind man that helped the people in the town of River's Edge. Sheriff Ray White went to all the benefits to raise money for people in need. He served at the soup kitchen every Thanksgiving and Christmas, and Jake served right along with his father. If he saw anyone on the street that did not have a home, he would stop and take them to the local River's Edge homeless shelter and made sure they were given a shower, new clothes, a coat, a hot meal, and a place to sleep.

His father also held many fundraisers to keep the shelter up and running so that no one had to sleep outside in the River's Edge Community. He made sure no one was outside without a place to eat or sleep. He had felt such pride in his father because he helped so many people. No matter what *The Reaper* said, he would never change his mind about his dad. In his eyes, his father was a *hero*, not an "omen" of death that he had read about earlier that day.

Ryan Happer

Besides "The Lottery," there were many other books on each shelf that referenced the conflict of good versus evil. That was the underlying theme of the entire collection. One gruesome story in particular was entitled "The Omen," in which a boy had been born as the devil incarnate. He was pure evil, but his parents realized that fact much too late. Parents never want to believe in the vile tendencies that may be prevalent at a young age.

Ryan didn't believe in spiritual possession of the devil. Although he was positive the devil existed as he was a believer in God, he felt that evil was a choice. "Hope will shine its light and the darkness will flee!" Ryan had prayed for hope and that was what God had bestowed upon him.

Ernie Jr.

Sitting on the bed as he ate his breakfast, Ernie was reading another short story entitled "A Good Man Is Hard to Find." It was almost as shocking as the other stories in the repertoire left for him to peruse. Jesus Christ, what in the hell was wrong with people? If any of these works of fiction had been based on the true dark nature of life, then Ernie was certain the devil really was alive and well residing in the hearts and souls of humanity.

In the book, a family takes a vacation. The author makes it very clear that the mother, father, and two children already know that their grandma is going to be annoying.

As they are driving, a news program warns everyone that three men have broken out of jail. The warning is especially frightening due to the fact that they are coldblooded killers.

While the family heads to the beach, the grandmother speaks up and tells them that she remembers the road they are on and asks her son to take her to her old house so that she can see it one last time. The family is frustrated, but her son does start down the dirt road toward the house that his mother is talking about. All of a sudden, the grandmother realizes she has made a mistake but does not tell her family because she knows they will all be angry with her. After looking at the house that is falling apart because no one has lived there in years, they all sit down to have a picnic under a shade tree.

That's when they hear the noise. Suddenly, three men come down the little hill to where the family was eating. They seem friendly at first. But the grandmother makes the mistake of letting them know who they are; she blurts out, "You are the three that escaped from the prison!"

The leader of the three just shakes his head. The grandmother says, "You won't hurt us, I know. You are a good man. I can see it in your eyes."

Two of the men take the father and the little boy farther into the field, and two gunshots are heard. Then they come back and take the mother and daughter. Again, two shots go off. Then the leader of the group bends down eye to eye with the grandmother, who is now crying because she has realized this is all her fault.

"Ma'am, I have been called many names in my life but 'good' is not one of them." Then he pulls out his gun and shoots her in the head.

Ernie's video games were violent but not as sinister as these tales of horror. He threw the book across the room as hard as he could. His New York Yankees hat fell off of his head and the book bounced off the wall. There it lay open on the floor, as if calling to him with some unknown force. Ernie felt like a mechanical robot crossing the room to retrieve the collection that portrayed such bizarre accounts of unequivocal terror.

Chapter Forty-Nine
The Next Move
Present Day

The last seven envelopes were now placed in each mailbox. Each one contained the choice they would all need to make to save their children. It was a decision that would need to be carried out by the entire *pack*. If even one of the seven refused the terms and conditions provided within, then the four innocents would be put to death. They, like Madeline, would never have the pleasure of knowing another Halloween, birthday, or Christmas. *The pack* had to believe he meant every word he said so they would all confess to the murder of Madeline Singer.

Driving through the streets of River's Edge, he wondered if the parents had read his final instructions as of yet. He wondered if they would remember what they had done to a beautiful young girl who would have grown into a magnificent human being. He believed with all his heart that Madeline would have done something wonderful with her life, making the world become a better place.

Gripping the steering wheel tight enough that the whites of his knuckles were drawn taut against his skin, the anger came again like a tidal wave. Damn them! They *should* remember! They *should* remember every horrible moment of what they had done.

Pulling off to the side of the road, he opened his car door and put his head between his knees. He knew this wave of crippling emotion would pass.

Sometimes it felt as though his brain was about to pop out of his skull. Would these episodes of panic finally cease when he achieved his goal? Because one way or another, his plan would come to fruition. He had played the game to win. No matter what *the pack* chose to do, there *would* be justice for Madeline.

Leaning back against the car seat, he centered his mind and began to breathe slowly, in and out, in and out, in and out. Eyes closed, he counted each breath until he gained control again because he would need unyielding control for the next part of the plan. His mind drifted away to a time when he was young. Madeline was smiling, laughing, running, going down the slide at school. The school was hideous, but Madeline made it shine like a diamond. When she was around it seemed as though the town held something more than it did; she made it beautiful. The town was just as horrid as it was twenty-five years ago. When she was murdered, in his mind, they had taken away the only part of the town that had meaning and the truest beauty he had ever seen.

Chapter Fifty
A New Player
Present Day

The plane had just touched down very late at night in Cincinnati, Ohio. Although it had been an easy flight, the older man felt as if the turbulence they had experienced was now settled deep into his chest.

Grabbing his luggage and heading to the rent a car area had caused his breathing to become heavy. On top of his graying hair sat a black fedora, which shadowed the deepest blue of his eyes. His tailored coat was also black, along with the leather satchel that hung from his shoulder.

Staring straight ahead, his eyes were transfixed as though he might be on a mission of great importance.

Pulling slowly out of the parking lot, he turned the silver sedan in the direction of River's Edge, KY. Heart hammering in his chest as every mile seemed to go by at a snail's pace, bringing him closer and closer to the past. His heart rate was at a high level and his hands shook as he drove the car to the place he thought he would never see again. But when he had gotten the call, he knew he had to come. His mind went in and out of memories. It was hard to keep his mind from straying. Sometimes his mind would sink so deep into a memory he would almost forget that he was driving and he would have to remember why he was coming back to River's Edge.

Chapter Fifty-one
Bad Dreams
Present Day

Vera Tate

Vera's dreams had been dominated by death for the past few nights. In each dream she was running through the streets of the town. She ran as fast as her chubby legs would carry her, continuing to trip over the undergrowth that was growing at a high intensity. The sharp vines cut and tore her pink-and-white waitress uniform with each hurried step.

Although she was positive she was in the town that she grew up in, everything looked completely different to her. All the houses had fallen in on themselves and the trees and shrubs had begun to take over; their branches grew crooked and wild, reaching out for her in every direction.

The sky burned a crimson red as if heaven itself was bleeding. Blood dripped out of the illuminated scarlet dome over her head. It oozed onto the tree that was standing before her, *the hanging tree*. Although she tried to run away from the tree, she could not escape its ever-looming presence. Each path she chose brought her back to the exact same spot in front of the gnarled monstrosity in which a body hung from one of its crooked limbs.

When the dream began she was always her adult self, but then a metamorphosis occurred within her body, changing her to the younger form of her being. Once the change would occur there was nowhere to run. The foliage blocked her path no matter where she turned. Suddenly, a thunderous voice would echo from the blood-soaked sky. This time, it commanded her to look up at the lifeless form hanging above her head. Her eyes were pulled up by an unseen magnet to the skeletal remains of Madeline Singer.

Vera screamed in terror as she tried to tear herself away from the decomposing corpse. But her feet were entangled by the roots of the tree and it held her there as if nature was demanding her confession of what she had done so long ago.

At the end of the dream the skeleton changed in shape until it wasn't Madeline hanging on the end of the rope. It was Vera *herself*, her brown eyes bulging from their sockets, the elongated tongue hanging from her open mouth. Her face was stone-cold white and the tongue that hung open from her mouth was black as coal. Blood dripped all the way down her body. She swayed back and forth from the noose around her neck as the wind started to pick up and the tree limbs began to sway as well. Back on the ground with her feet tangled in the foliage, she saw the most horrible thing of all. There were no eyes in the swaying corpse. Just sockets staring at her. Blood running down her face. Then the corpse moaned. On and on it moaned and the wind was blowing harder.

She tried to pull her feet out of the mud and limbs that were trapping her there to witness herself hanging from the tree. Vera's screaming finally came to an end when the ground beneath her opened up and swallowed her whole. When she woke up in her own bed she ran to the bathroom and emptied the contents of her stomach over and over again. Until there was nothing left. She held on to the toilet while sweat popped out over her entire body as she started to cry. Her mother was asleep so there was no one to comfort her. And, even if her mother were awake she would just tell her to stop that dumbass crying and go to bed.

Then a thought crossed her decaying mind. She had not looked at the mail today. She walked to the slot in the door. She couldn't believe her eyes. There was a form to fill out for the *Publishers Clearing House Sweepstakes*. She went to the table in the kitchen and filled out the form like she had for so many years. Horrible thoughts came and went as she completed the entry. The fact that she had an inkling that she might just win this time showed she was beginning to drift further into insanity.

Sheriff Ray White

Sheriff White was so sleep deprived that he had begun to nod off while looking at the latest evidence collected by the CISVU. It was early in the morning on the 29th of October that he had the worst panic attack he had experienced in twenty-five years.

While waiting for Brian Caster to get to the station for the interview with Helen Marks, Ray had closed his eyes to shut out the pictures of the four teenagers that lined the evidence board. His hefty frame slid wearily into the chair next to him and he drifted into a deeply agonizing nightmare that took him back in time.

When he opened his eyes, he was standing on the bank of the Ohio River with the entire pack around him. He was in the middle of the group and the other six were chanting something as they circled, ready to strike. Their huge blood-red eyes fixated on him while they repeated the same words: "Gay Ray, Gay Ray, Gay Ray...."

Suddenly, he wasn't in the middle of the circle anymore. He had become one of *the pack*, who were continuing to chant as they moved stealth-like around the boy that stood in the middle of the circle with his eyes full of fear.

Ray squinted hard to try and see who had now replaced him as a target. Confusion clouded his brain for a few seconds, because the boy they had trapped still looked like him. When the realization hit him, it dropped him to his knees. It was his son standing there! Oh, God, Jake was in the middle of that deadly circle.

He had to save him. Ray knew exactly what was going to happen if he didn't do something to stop it now.

He ran into the inner circle and screamed at Jake to RUN! He screamed it several times until Jake finally did run out of the circle. The other members of *the pack* began to circle him. They were taunting, leering with saliva dripping from their mouths. He watched them warily as the space between them began to get closer to him. They growled like hungry animals. Each of them had huge sharp fingernails that shone in the light of the moon. Ernie reached out and scratched him and made a deep cut on his face. The rest of *the pack* howled at the light of the full moon. Todd came from behind and made five deep cuts into Ray's back and he cried out. The other six laughed and laughed like hyenas. In his ear Todd whispered, "Gay Bait, you piece of shit."

"Not *the shit* like we are! Just a pathetic piece of rotting shit."

Then Ernie pulled Jake back into the circle and said, "Like father, like son." Now he and Jake were both in the circle together.

"Jake, I will not let them hurt you! I will never let them hurt you! I will never let them hurt anyone ever again."

Ray slowly reached for his gun and in a split second his hand was on the trigger. "If you dare hurt my son, I will kill you where you stand. You will never lay a hand on anyone again!"

However, *the pack* laughed and moved forward. They cackled and taunted him. "RUN!" he screamed at the top of his lungs.

"RUN, JAKE, RUN NOW!" he screamed even louder as he pulled the gun ready to fire at *the pack* that continued to circle him.

"You are the biggest coward in the world, Ray. You could never pull that trigger. Why don't you give that to a real man," Ernie walked toward him and Ray shot him in the head. The rest of them ran for their lives. For if Ray was capable of killing Ernie, then he was capable of killing them as well.

Ray called for his son, "Jake, where are you? JAKE! JAKE! JAKE!"

At that moment he awoke from his horrifying dream. His body fell out of the chair when he screamed his son's name. The jolt brought him back to his senses. He was lying on the floor of the police station, gasping for air, when Alicia Davidson burst into the room.

"Sheriff White, are you okay?" Her voice was shrill as she kneeled down beside him. "Call 911!" she barked at the receptionist, who was standing at the door.

Ray had enough energy to point to the inhaler that had skidded across the room when he had fallen. Alicia retrieved it, held it to his mouth pumping twice, and he inhaled as much of the mist that he could, forcing it into his lungs.

Tabitha Preston
Because Tabitha was taking nerve medication like candy, her hazy stupor brought her in and out of consciousness. She had retreated to her bedroom after the visit from Reese; Ernie had stayed down in the living room staring at the fire.

The neighbors were taking turns sitting with her, bringing her food that she did not eat, holding her hand during the silent hours of morning, just before dawn would break across the sky.

Ernie Sr. was lost in his own world of vengeance and fury. Too preoccupied with revenge to pay Tabitha any attention. So, she lay in the bed drifting in her own distorted dream world from which she could not escape.

The worst dream had been one in which she was encased in a glass casket. She wore a beautiful white gown with glowing gemstones. A necklace of brilliant diamonds was around her neck. Her long chestnut hair fell upon the satin white pillow. She could see herself lying there as plain as day. Then the vision shifted to a different perspective. Her spirit was now captive in the glass case along with her physical body. She tried to open her eyes, but they seemed to be glued shut.

Tabitha tried to scream but her mouth would not open to form the words. She was going to be buried alive; six feet under the ground for eternity. The worms would crawl and wiggle around her in the depths of hell.

She could hear people talking as they gathered around the coffin to say their last farewell. In her mind she screamed, *I'm alive. Don't do this, I'm alive!*

No one could hear her as she lay paralyzed from the rest of the world.

Hearing her father's voice caused a sob to wrench across her heart. "She's pretty as a picture," he said before moving away to another part of the room.

"I'm alive!" she screamed with all her might, but the words were not coming out. "I am right here!" she cried louder.

Then Ernie Sr. walked over and smiled at her. "Nothing that a little glue won't fix, Tabbs. I just gave you enough of those little pills to put you asleep for a while. Glued your mouth. Good Lord, you just never stop talking, you stupid bitch. I should have done this a very long time ago. Now you are going in the ground, six feet under, and that is where you will meet your end. Oh and don't ever bother trying to move or speak. I gave you something that would cause paralysis as well. So just lay there and think about what kind of a death you are going to meet, my dear. By the way, I did receive those divorce papers and, well, seventy-five percent just wasn't enough. I want it all!"

Suddenly, her dream switched to her own swimming pool in the backyard of her house. She was in the middle of the pool and *the pack* was moving around her. Their eyes were black as coal and they were hissing like snakes. They began to get into the swimming pool. She tried to get out, but it was too late. Tabitha was in the circle and they were reaching out to grab her, and they started to hold her head beneath the water as she thrashed to no avail. She knew this was the end. It was her fate. There were too many to fight off. In her dream, Tabitha died in her swimming pool as she pulled the water deep into her lungs.

At last, Tabitha awoke from the torturous nightmare; her screams could be heard all over the house. Poor Mrs. Prescott was on "Tabatha watch" that night had to smack Tabitha to calm her down. It did help her, but she was shaking so hard and the panic came on so fast Tabitha thought she might be having a heart attack from all the stress she had been under in the last few days. Mrs. Prescott gave her a pill that was on her nightstand that helped her with the panic attack, and finally she calmed down enough that she began to fall asleep again in a peaceful slumber. Mrs. Prescott gently rubbed Tabitha's head as she went back to sleep and told her everything was going to be okay. Then she pulled Tabitha into her arms and rocked her back and forth just as her mother might have done if she hadn't left her so long ago, when she was just a little girl. Tabitha let Mrs. Prescott hold her. For the first time in a long time Tabitha felt safe.

Ernie Johnson Sr.
His wife's screams didn't faze him. He stared into the fire while taking a long sip of an expensive glass of vodka. Ernie didn't have nightmares anymore; he had slept like a baby for many, many years. Once he had killed both of his parents, at the age of eighteen, his nights were filled with a long, restful sleep.

He had made it look like his father had killed his mother and then shot himself in the head. All he had to do was put the gun in this father's hand. Everyone believed it; he knew they would. What a load of shit! His father didn't have the guts to use a gun. But, he'd born a son who did have the balls to confront and conquer any obstacle placed in his life. That's how he had seen his parents, like an obstacle that needed to be eradicated. He remembered the shock on their faces when he walked in with the gun. His mother on another drinking spree and his father with the cocaine abuse. When his mother saw the gun she whimpered like a sick dog and cowered in the corner of the kitchen. His father tried the most ludicrous thing of all. Told Ernie that they loved him so much, that they had from the time he was a baby. Then Ernie lifted his shirt and showed them the scars from what they had been doing to him over his entire life. Scars that would never heal.

"You have hit me for the last time." He shot his mother in the head first and turned to his father, who was begging for his life, and shot him in the head as well. Ernie knew how to place the gun to make it a murder-suicide. He donned gloves to make sure there were none of his fingerprints on the gun. Then he placed the gun in his father's hand, took the gloves off, and put them in his pocket.

He was eighteen years old when the crime was committed and considered an adult, capable of taking care of himself. No foster homes for him. It was torture having to wait so long to be old enough to kill them. But it was done, and Ernie was finally free of the two people he hated most in the world. Then they were cremated and turned into ash.

The only people he ever really cared about, besides himself, were Tabitha and Ernie Jr. Although Ernie Sr. couldn't feel any kind of real emotion, other than anger and darkness, he knew those two were as close as he would ever get to what some people might call love.

His thoughts drifted into a wakeful dream, what he would do to *The Reaper* when he found him. He stroked the gun in his lap and thought about pulling the trigger if what John said was true. If a member from *the pack* was playing this little game, he would bring hellfire down on them like they had never seen before.

Ernie still had not become fully aware of the situation in which he had been placed. A life of pure dominance continued to feed his delusion of control. He was now away from the constant bullying from his mother and his father. However, Ernie didn't know what kind of terror that was coming his way this time.

Todd Barker
Todd and his wife, Amy, were lying on the king-sized bed in the master suite of their home. He'd rubbed Amy's back until she had fallen asleep and he had finally nodded off himself. All of a sudden, he was in the emergency room preparing to do emergency surgery on a patient that was bleeding internally. Once he was scrubbed, he walked into the surgical quarters, which housed the patient, two nurses, and an anesthesiologist. On the gurney lay a young girl. Looking closer he recognized the face of Madeline Singer. My God, he was getting the chance to save her. He said to his team, "We are going to use everyone and everything possible to save this girl!"

She flatlined before he could even begin the surgical procedure that might save her life. He used the paddles to shock her back to life again and again. The nurse pronounced her dead as Dr. Todd Barker continued to send shockwaves through her body, intent on bringing her back to life.

The nurse touched his arm in an effort to stop his fruitless effort, but he was adamant about saving her. "Come on, Madeline! Come on!" he repeated in utter exhaustion. He continued to use the shockwaves and pump her heart over and over. He would not give up. He worked on her for over thirty minutes but he could not bring her back.

When he had finally given up, he looked down at her face. But, it wasn't Madeline lying dead on the metallic silver table; it was his Katie Girl! "Oh,

God, noooooo! Noooooo!" he cried as he held his daughter's cold and lifeless body in his arms. "Don't take my baby girl. Please, I will trade my life for hers. No…. No…. God, nooooooooo!"

Tears slipped down his cheeks. When he looked at the corpse again, it was Madeline he held in his arms. He kept trying to revive her over and over again. His team had gone home. "Come on, Madeline, come on, you can do this…I know you can!" After so many times of trying to bring her back, he was exhausted with sweat running down his face.

When Todd awoke from his asleep, he was shouting, "I can do this. Just give me time. I can bring her back. I know I can. I am a surgeon, by God!"

Finally, after what seemed like an hour, he awoke from his dream and his wife was holding him in her arms. They held on to each other the rest of the night. Todd could not sleep before morning had dawned. Remembering what they had done to Madeline so many years ago gave him the shakes for over an hour.

John Happer

Staring at the ceiling, John replayed the events his mind had created like a horror movie. He'd fallen asleep in the wee hours of morning, hoping to escape reality for a bit. The joint helped with that endeavor, but it most likely helped to conjure up the images that were now burned in his brain as well.

He and Paul were thirteen again, sitting in the front pew listening to their dad speak to the congregation. Then suddenly the cross went up in a blaze of fire everyone ran *helter-skelter* for the exit. They knocked each other down in an attempt to get out of the tinder box that was going up in smoke. People were trampled to death as the strong overtook the weak in a white-hot frenzy.

John was frozen in complete shock as the fire rampaged out of control. Finally, coming to his senses, he ran for the door, stepping on the dead bodies in an attempt to get himself out alive.

When he reached the front door, he heard Paul shout his name. Turning back toward the flames he saw that a beam had fallen on his brother, pinning his legs to the floor. Without thought, he went back for Paul. He tried with all of his might to lift the wooden plank off of his brother, but it was no use.

"Get out!" Paul screamed. "Go, leave me!"

Reverend Thomas Happer cradled both boys in his arms and welcomed the fiery ending to his life. His father kept repeating, "I love you, boys. I love you so much. There is no greater love than a parent has for his child. I want you to understand that. And, God's love is one hundred times greater than that."

Paul Happer
Paul walked into the bedroom and sat down on the side of the bed. It was so small that John's long legs stretched out over the end of the mattress.

"Bad dream?" John asked, looking into the eyes of his brother. They usually had the same dreams. Especially when they were in a great deal of stress.

"There was a fire. I was trapped; you tried to save me."

"But, I couldn't."

Paul shook his head. "Neither could Dad. So, you both burned with me."

"I'm with you till the end."

"It felt like he knew. Like he knew what we had done."

"Yes, it did feel that way," agreed John.

"If he does know, then why hasn't he said anything? Why didn't he make us confess?"

"He's protected us. All this time he's protected us from our sins. Just like any father would do, Paul. You would do anything to save Ryan, wouldn't you?"

Paul nodded and the twins sat together in silence. Jesus came out of the clock to give his hourly blessing. And, somewhere in the stillness of that moment both of the Happer twins found God.

Chapter Fifty-two

The Beast About to Strike

Twenty-five Years Ago – All Hallows' Eve

The seven members of *the pack* circled around Madeline with menacing smiles on their faces. They made fun of her princess dress and pushed her to the ground several times.

After the fourth time she stayed down, in the hopes that they would leave her alone. Ernie grabbed her by the hair and dragged her up onto her feet. Holding her with one arm, he pulled her long dress up over her head with the other. *The pack* growled in laughter at her flowery pink underwear.

When he let her go he tried pushing her to the ground again, but she caught herself and ran for her life. She could hear them pursuing like wild dogs as she ran toward Front Street. She was so terrified that her legs carried her through the town without a thought of where she was headed.

In a blind panic, tears running down her cheeks, she raced down the bank of the Ohio River below. She was at the water's edge before the realization that she was trapped. *The pack* closed in on all sides, eyes boiling over with a demonic hatred. She screamed and cried out hoping that someone would hear her words and save her from *the pack*. But the adults in River's Edge seemed as though a cloud had come over them and thought the screaming was just another prank conjured up for Halloween fun.

Chapter Fifty-three

Another Guest

Present Day

The silver car angled along the paved driveway that took him up the incline leading to the *house on the hill*. He pulled into the four-car garage and turned off the engine. For a long while he could not bring himself to get out of the car.

Seeing the house flooded him with memories of Madeline. Her smiling face, her wondrous loving spirit, and her grounded intellect of an old soul that looked upon life as a beautiful adventure. When she was a little girl, he'd played many games of hide-and-seek in this house, pretending that he couldn't find her. Then, acting scared when she jumped out to reveal herself, giggling at the thought of outsmarting him. Little songs they would sing together with her mother. Baking cookies for the holidays, birthday surprises, long talks about interesting subjects, and her love of helping people. So many beautiful traits of Madeline!

He had lived twenty-five long years without knowing what had happened to her that night. It had almost driven him to the point of insanity.

Finally, he opened the car door, retrieved his satchel and walked toward the house with a determined gate; steeling himself for the hours that lay ahead. He must do this, for Madeline!

The Reaper opened the door as the man ascended the steps.

Chapter Fifty-four

Together Again: Take Two

Present Day

Hours later *the pack* sat in Vera Tate's dilapidated living room because her house was the only one that was not under surveillance by the police.

Ernie paced the floor like a cobra ready to strike.

Tabitha sat on one end of the worn-out yellow couch with her hands in her lap as had been her usual posture for the past few days. However, she had not taken a nerve pill since the last nightmare had sent her over the edge. Her screams had lasted until Mrs. Jamison, the next-door neighbor, had finally slapped her again across the face to bring her out of the hysterics. Mrs. Jamison just happened to be the unlucky person on "Tabitha Watch" that morning. And all the while, Ernie Sr. remained unmoving in his armchair by the fire. His cronies still had nothing to report about *The Reaper*.

John and Paul Happer sat together on the spotted yellow-and-white loveseat that had seen better days. Paul pulled relentlessly at a piece of thread that was coming loose from the arm of the sofa.

Sheriff White was leaning against the doorway that led into the small brown and orange kitchen. His arms were folded over his broad chest.

Dr. Todd Barker leaned against the wall, looking as if a tiny wind might blow him into oblivion.

Vera sat with Tabitha on the couch, which caused it to tilt in her direction. Tabitha was surprised that the couch hadn't already collapsed under the extreme weight of Vera Tate. *Extreme weight of Vera Tate*, she thought again. That rhymes! God, what was wrong with her? She was slowly but surely losing her mind. They all were.

They decided to read this one together. Each member of *the pack* read the typed message and a deadly silence filled the room. Then, all hell broke loose.

Chapter Fifty-Five

The Visitor

Present Day

When *He* opened the door to his new houseguest, the man entering stumbled as if in great pain. *The Reaper* caught him just before he hit the floor, helping him to a dusty cloth-covered chair that was once grand in both elegance and splendor.

The years had swept through the old mansion, wreaking havoc in their wake. Cobwebs hung from the ceiling, the paint was cracked and careworn, and each piece of furniture that used to decorate the home sat abandoned and aging just like the old man in the black fedora. The only new items were all the Halloween decorations.

The Reaper let the man gain his composure. "Are you all right, Doc?"

Doc continued to try and catch his breath. "Yes, just give me a minute to get my bearings."

When Doc finally stood up he looked around the house slowly, moving from one piece of covered furniture to another, laying a hand on each piece as if trying to "feel" the emotions harbored within the wood and the stuffing that sat underneath each dust-riddled cover.

Finally, his eyes met the man standing solemnly beside him. There was concern in those eyes. "I'm all right, son. No need to worry about an *old codger* like me."

The Reaper's mouth turned slightly upward in a smile of supreme fondness for the old codger. "If you're not up to this, I certainly understand."

"Are you *certain* that it will need to be done?"

"Yes, sir."

Doc nodded absentmindedly, his thoughts meandering to happier times in the *house on the hill*.

He looked at *The Reaper* in surprise as he walked toward the mantle. His hand was shaking as he took down one of the poems that had been framed. This and the other poem were the only items free of dust in the room.

When he looked up he had tears in his eyes. "You kept these for me all these years?"

"Of course I did, Doc. I knew that you left them behind because Mrs. Singer was coming apart at the seams and any great personal effects from Madeline might be too much for her at the time. However, I knew the day would come when you would want them back. To have a piece of her soul and how she felt about you, Doc."

After looking at the poem in his hand for several moments, he began to read the poem that Madeline had given him for Father's Day when she was eleven years old. His hand was shaking and there were tears in his voice as he read the poem out loud:

My Hero

Every little boy
Dreams of hitting that homerun
As the crowd roars his name
And chants, "You're number ONE!"

Every little boy
Has dreams of his own
Of leading his team to victory
As that World Series ball is thrown.

Throughout these dreams
The hero saves the day!
He shines so brightly
And always leads the way.

*But little boys grow up
And most raise families.
Sometimes they forget
What they dreamed to be.*

*They become daddies
Have children of their own
The world will never know
That he **DID** become a **HERO!***

*To a little girl with long blonde hair
Who thinks he hung the moon
And put the stars up in the sky
To dance a lovely tune*

*He throws her in the air
And lets her follow him around.
Makes her laugh, gives her advice
Tells her that he's proud.*

*Proud to be her daddy
Because he loves her so!
I love you too, Dad,
Thanks for being my **HERO!!***

Written for "my" dad

– Madeline Singer

Doc wiped his eyes. "Thank you so much for keeping this for me. You have no idea how much it means. I'd almost forgotten about this poem. I think I can finally take it home now and sit it on my mantle."

Placing his poem back, he took the other one down and began to read it out loud as well. Madeline had given this one to her mother on Mother's Day of the same year:

My Hero

When I think about the person
That I want to be
Images come to mind
Beautiful memories,
A memory of a little girl
Sitting on her mommy's lap.
And Mommy holding her so tight
As she takes a peaceful nap.

A memory of a celebration
A beautiful dress so new.
I said, "I love you, Mommy."
She said, "I love you, too."

Then there was the costume ball
Where a little girl lost the prize.
And Mommy hugging her so tight
Saying "To me you'll ALWAYS SHINE!"

These memories in my heart
Of a woman like no other.
When I think about the person I would like to be
It's you I think of, Mother!

Written for "my" mom

– Madeline Singer

    "My little girl was so talented," Doc said through the tears running down his face. I know she would have been a wonderful woman. She had a beautiful spirit and a beautiful heart. Ripped from the world too soon. Taken from us! Dear God! My sweet little girl!"

    Doc broke down in heaving sobs. *The Reaper* helped him to one of the old couches in the huge dusty room and sat down beside him. Both of them cried together for the loss that had been taken away from them for twenty-five years.

Chapter Fifty-six
Something Wicked This Way Comes
Present Day

Ernie Jr.
The Picture of Dorian Gray was the book that Ernie Jr. had just finished reading. He was now staring at the wall opposite the small bed in the chamber room. Rocking back and forth, seemingly catatonic, his thoughts were encumbered by the horrific images the books on the shelves had plastered forever within his young mind.

God Almighty, why in the hell did he keep reading these dark tales? They were leading him into the depths of hell itself. He couldn't stop the onslaught of terror that kept coming at him like a runaway train, feeding his imagination with cryptic thoughts of his parents, which were hanging like a spider's web, determined to finish off the prey unlucky enough to get caught in those sticky threads.

This book centered on a man who allowed evil to grow within the pages of his life by making a deal with the devil. Ernie Jr. had decided it must be Satan with whom Dorian Gray had made the deal, giving up his soul to remain young and beautiful, forever. The picture of Dorian turned grotesque and vile while the man himself was untouched by the hands of illness or age.

Each time Dorian uncovered the painting, more of his soul was displayed in horrific earnestness on the ever-changing canvas—a graphic madness that was his true selfish, murderous being.

Although the book was centered on a male protagonist, Ernie's thoughts continued to drift toward the *grandiose picture of his mother* hanging perfectly on the wall above the decorated fireplace in the great room of their home....

Ryan Happer
Ryan knew *The Reaper* was trying to educate them between living in the dark verses the light. He had just finished *Something Wicked This Way Comes*, a book about a carnival that comes to town with a foreshadowing of bringing evil along for the ride. The images that the book conjured were overpowering. Ryan grabbed the *Bible* and held it tightly to his chest.

As the carousel turned vividly in his own mind, it became covered in blood. It ran down the merry-go-round ponies as if it would never end. And Ryan knew this blood was connected to innocence lost. What had their parents done? It had to be something horrific. And, he knew two things for sure. His dad was connected to the angel in white. In his gut he also knew they all their parents were linked to the murder everyone talked about as a ghost story that was linked with the *house on the hill*. But, it was no ghost story. No, it was a true story and their parents had been involved. While pacing back and forth, tears fell from his eyes and the sins of his father, whatever they were, became seared in his brain forever.

Katie Barker
"The Tell-Tale Heart" by Edgar Allan Poe had always fascinated Katie, a man driven insane from his own sin of committing murder, and then burying the victim beneath his very own house. The dead heart continued to beat its rhythm of guilt, driving the killer insane.

Sometimes she felt as though she might be going insane, locked in this room on the *house on the hill*. She paced the floor and felt as if a steady heartbeat was under her feet, filling her head with dark images of murder. It seemed as the days went on, the heartbeat got louder and louder under the floor until she realized it was her own heart beating rapidly and playing tricks on her otherwise logical brain.

Jake White
Something Wicked This Way Comes fell from Jake's hand and landed with a thump on the floor by the bed. His head was reeling with the sights and sounds of the wicked images conjured by a carnival that had come to a small

Midwestern town one warm October night, when the moon always seemed to shine more brightly and there was a crisp sound in the air as shoes crunched over the beautiful falling leaves. The brightly lit carousel could grant wishes to its patrons. However, each wish came with great cost. Riding forward would allow you to become older if you wished to escape all childhood and teenage years of teasing and humiliation you knew might be coming your way. However, spinning backward fulfilled a wish most desirable to all older people again searching for their youth. Hoping to take all the wisdom with them that they had learned over the years and not make the same mistakes as when "nature's first green was gold."

The carnival provided the promise of wishes to be fulfilled. For no one understood the price for riding the carousel was giving up your soul to the devil himself.

Chapter Fifty-seven
No Way Out
Present Day – October 30th

After *the pack* read the letters addressed to all seven members, everyone began talking at once except for Vera; she knew that this was coming all along.

Ernie Johnson was pacing the floor like a madman and had been doing so since they had all opened their letters.

Sheriff White read out loud the words that were on each letter. "You murdered Madeline Singer twenty-five years ago. This is your twenty-fifth anniversary of living free lives as murderers in River's Edge. By twelve midnight on October 31st, you will either confess to the murder of Madeline Singer or your own children will be murdered. Innocent blood spilled again will be left on your hands because you have the power to save them just as you had the power to save Madeline all those years ago. Because you are a *pack*, you must confess as a *pack*. If one of the seven members who used to call themselves *the shit* so many years ago does not confess to this murder, all of your children will be killed. So, think carefully about your decision. At least I am giving you a choice. One that Madeline's mother and father never had while *the pack* murdered their daughter and hung her from a tree. Make no mistake, 'you're all in this together, bitches!'"

"How in the hell did he know that last line?" asked Paul Happer.

"What do you mean?" spat Ernie.

Paul rose from the sofa. "What I mean is that those are the last words you said to us about what we did that night. Ray wanted to go to the police and you shoved him to the ground, pulled out a knife, and said, 'We're all in this together, bitches.' One big, happy fucking family. How could anyone else know that except the seven of us?"

The pack got very quiet for a moment as they thought through what Paul had said. Could a member of *the pack* be *The Reaper*? But why?

John leaned forward on the couch. "Either someone was listening that night or *The Reaper* is in this room right now."

"Son of a bitch!" shouted Ernie. "I don't know what kind of game this reaper thinks he is playing, but I am out. No one is going to tell me what to do!! If it is one of you and find out, you are as good as dead!!!!

Paul Happer moved closer to Ernie. "What exactly do you mean you are out?"

"I am not confessing to anything!" he spat.

And that was when it happened. Paul Happer flew across the room and tackled Ernie to the ground. Paul let his rage consume him and he beat Ernie Johnson to what seemed like an inch of his life. *No one stopped him.*

Chapter Fifty-eight
This Little Piggy
Present Day

In the *house on the hill*, Doc was preparing for a special kind of surgery. Removing a body part from a thirteen-year-old boy was giving him the shakes, but he knew it had to be done. He believed in *The Reaper*. Had all of his life. If *The Reaper* felt this was the only way to get a confession out of the seven people who had killed his daughter, then he would be strong and move ahead as planned.

Ernie Jr. was lying unconscious on an operating table. The boy had no memory of having been brought to this sterile room in the house. A surgical room that had everything the doctor would need to carry out the procedure.

Each of the four rooms had been equipped with a small air tube at the top of the ceiling so that a certain type of gas could be pumped in if needed. This gas was what put Ernie to sleep so that he could be transported to the surgical room in the *house on the hill* for the amputation of his right pinkie toe.

The toe had been chosen because it had a very predominant birthmark. A large part of the skin on the toe was red. And when *the package* was delivered to them, there would be no mistaking to Ernie Sr. and Tabitha that it belonged to Ernie Jr. *The Reaper* knew that Ernie Johnson Sr. would be the hardest one to get a confession from and that extreme measures would need to be taken to get him to talk.

So, Doc worked alone in the surgical room because *The Reaper* had somewhere else he had to be to continue and carry out the plan.

When the toe was removed, Doc kept the toe on ice to make sure it could be replaced but time was of the essence. He made sure to take good care of Ernie Jr. with expert care. For he knew that it was not this boy's fault what his father had done. As Doc wheeled the surgical bed back to Ernie Jr.'s room, he shook his head and thought; *the sins of the father*.

Chapter Fifty-nine

Just When You Think You Know
Present Day – October 30th

As Paul was hitting Ernie with blow after blow, Tabitha Preston snapped out of her stupor, jumped up, and ran to both of them.

Grabbing Paul's arm, she pleaded for him to stop, "He saved me!" she cried. Over and over she shouted the words until Paul let Ernie fall to the floor in a bloody mess.

Vera was crying as well. During the fight they had broken almost all of her treasured items. Though she didn't have many, there were a few that she cherished that were now in pieces on the floor. Precious ornaments that she had collected over the years, her ceramic bear collection was now lying all over the floor. But, nobody cared about Vera. She was the only one alone in this nightmare. Breaking all of her beautiful things that she had worked so hard for made her fall in upon herself as she cried softly at the drama playing out in her living room.

"Tabitha," said Paul. "What in the hell are you talking about? He treats you like shit all of the time. He's never saved anybody but himself, and now he doesn't even want to save his own child!"

Tears fell from Tabitha's cheeks as she held a bloody, unconscious Ernie on her lap and looked up at *the pack*. "My brother, Anthony, was everything to my father. When he turned fifteen, my father began grooming him to take over the family business. What my father didn't know...," she trailed off and inhaled a big breath, bracing herself for what she knew she had to share now, or else the others would never understand, "...was that Anthony, who was four years older than me, started raping me when I was ten. I never told anyone. I was too ashamed.

"When Ernie and I got together, he walked in and saw what he was doing to me, only this time Anthony was holding a knife to my throat. Ernie went crazy. He beat Anthony nearly to death and then he took him up to the top of the power and electric company and dropped him off the highest ledge so it would look like he committed suicide. Ernie even crafted the suicide note in such a way that my dad never even questioned that it could have been murder.

So, you see, he saved me from a life of abuse. A life of that he continued to go through until he was eighteen!"

Paul Happer ran a hand over his face and said, "Jesus Christ!" while the rest of *the pack* stared in shocked, utter silence.

"I thought he committed suicide, Tabitha," John said softly.

Tabitha shook her head. "Ernie made the note to look like Anthony's handwriting. No one questioned the note or the explanation he gave for killing himself. Ernie wrote in the letter that Mom had left us and that Dad was putting too much pressure on him to eventually run the plant."

As Tabitha looked away from Ernie's mangled face she looked at each member of *the pack*. "My brother would have eventually killed me if Ernie hadn't stopped him. The abuse was getting worse and worse. I tried to tell my father, but he refused to listen." Tabitha turned back to Ernie, who was beginning to come around. "But Ernie, he saved me."

Chapter Sixty
This Little Piggy Never Came Home
October 30th, 2014

When Ernie Jr. woke up, he felt groggy and sick at his stomach. He tried to get out of his bed, but when he swung his legs over the side he felt a strong pain in his foot. He looked down to find it bandaged with a bit of blood seeping through.

As he was reaching over to take the bandage off, a voice came over the speaker in his room. "I wouldn't take that off just yet, son."

Ernie narrowed his eyes. "You're not *The Reaper*. Who are you? His partner?"

"I am a man here to tell you not to remove that bandage right now and to get back in the bed and try to sleep. If you try and walk right now, you are going to have a hard time and may pass out."

He began to unwrap the bandage. When he saw the horror of his toe missing, he started to scream his head off. What had they done to him? Was *The Reaper* really going to kill all of them if their parents didn't do what he wanted them to do!

Lightheadedness seized him suddenly. He didn't realize that the sleeping gas was coming through the tube to calm him down and put him to sleep. He fell back on the bed with the bandage in his hand.

Soon Doc entered Ernie Jr.'s room and wrapped up his foot and gave him a shot for the pain. Hopefully, it would help him sleep for a long while.

Chapter Sixty-one

A Special Delivery

Present Day

As *the pack* stood in stunned silence, the doorbell rang. They all jumped and looked wildly around at each other. It was decided Vera should answer her own door as if nothing unusual was happening, which was a complete understatement to Vera's way of thinking. They had broken almost all the pretty pieces of precious moments she had collected over the years, not to mention knocked down all her pictures and destroyed her living room when the fight broke out.

When Vera answered the door, a courier had a package that she needed to sign for. Thank God he didn't need to come inside the home, because she thought for sure he would call the police or tell someone even though Sheriff White was already there.

Ernie Johnson had regained consciousness and was sitting next to Tabitha on the sofa. He looked like he'd been hit by a tornado and he scowled at Paul, who simply smirked back.

The box the courier delivered was small with a white bow on top. It was addressed to *"The Pack"* and came with a nursery rhyme written was on the card: "This little Piggy went to market, this little piggy stayed home, this little piggy had roast beef, this little piggy had none, BUT, THIS LITTLE PIGGY WENT WEE, WEE, WEE ALL THE WAY HOME!"

The pack stared at the box as if it might explode at any minute. Sheriff White finally took the small box and opened it so that *the pack* could see what lay inside. A severed pinky toe with pink polish on the toenail, the same color Madeline Singer wore the night they had killed her.

Everyone jumped back from the box, repulsed; Vera ran to the bathroom to throw up. Paul and John turned away from the horrific sight. Sheriff White, Todd Barker, and Ernie stared at their future as if it had finally become clear in that one moment of certainty.

Tabitha was across the room screaming her head off and Todd Barker finally went over and held her. He took a syringe out of his bag and gave her a shot to calm her down.

Even though no words were spoken, the seven members of *the pack* knew they were headed to the River's Edge Police Station. And they would be confessing to the crime of murdering Madeline Singer in cold blood, twenty-five years ago.

Ernie Johnson walked around the room with his bloody cheek. "That could be a fake," he said.

Sheriff White grabbed him by the shirt. "My God! You complete psychopath! Your son's toe has been cut off!!!!"

Tabitha walked over to Ernie. "You know it's his, Ernie. It has his birthmark on it! We have to save him. It's our son, for God's sake."

Ernie stared at Ray, venom in his eyes. "How did you know it was Ernie's toe, Ray?"

Then there was a silence among *the pack* like there had never been before.

"I say we wait it out. We still have time. My men are still out there looking for this mad-man," Ernie breathed heavily.

Todd reached for the box. "Ernie, it's on ice. There might be a way to attach it back to his foot. But, we all need to go right now. We don't have much time."

Sheriff White pulled out his gun and said, "That is right. We don't have much time. Let's go, now!!!"

The pack was in complete shock as they stared at Ray's gun.

"You know you are a dead man walking, right, Ray?" Ernie snarled through his clenched teeth.

"Shut up, Ernie. I am so damn tired of you, it's taking every bit of willpower I have not to put a bullet in your head right now."

"Ray," said Tabitha.

"Shut your mouth, Tabitha. Because I am about ready to put one in your head, too. And, when we get there all of you are going to confess to everything that happened that night. The truth! The whole truth! If you even deviate one word from what happened, you will never see your children again! I said move. And, I mean now!"

Ray kept his gun on them the entire time. They all climbed into Ernie's black SUV. He told Paul to drive and had the others to get in with Ernie sitting right in front of him. He kept the gun trained on them.

"We're in this together, bitches. One big, happy fuckin' family. Right, Ernie?" Ray said.

Tabitha was crying andgarbled out, "Ray…how could…you do…this to…your ssssooonnnn…howw…could…you…do…this…to…our…child…."

"I said SHUT UP, Tabitha. You have no idea how hard it is not to pull this trigger right now." He placed the barrel of the gun to her head. "My God, I have wanted to do this for so long. If you don't shut up, I will blow your brains out. Or, maybe Paul should pull over and we could find the perfect rock, a jagged rock. How about that, Tabitha?"

"Oh, God…Ray…please…don't…," and she whimpered against the door.

"I seem to remember those words coming from another person. A sweet little thirteen-year-old girl. But, did it stop you? NO! So, I don't want to hear you crying, Tabitha. Do you understand me?"

He cocked the gun against her head and she reduced her crying so that no one could hear her.

Ernie turned to look at John and Ray blew a hole in the top of the SUV. Then he shot straight down the middle and blew out the windshield. Everyone jumped for cover. Like they could dodge a bullet if he really wanted to kill them.

"My God, Ray, you're going to kill us before we get there!" shouted John.

Ray still had the gun pointed toward the front of the SUV. "Paul, I asked you to drive for a reason. Tell me where we are going."

Paul raised his eyes and looked at Ray through the rearview mirror. "We're going to the police station, Ray."

They could feel the fury coming off of Ray's body and it was palpable, like heat waves, and they realized how truly serious he was with that gun in his hand.

Once they reached the station Ray put his gun away. He whispered to them again, "The truth, the whole truth, nothing but the truth. So help you God!"

Chapter Sixty-two
Blood Ties
Present Day

Ernie Jr.
Ernie Jr. was having the worst nightmare of his life. He was in a large forest and there were menacing eyes shining in the blackness all around him. Those eyes seemed to be getting closer and closer, and as Ernie turned to run he tripped over a branch and smacked his head against a tree. When he got to his feet, he realized the tree was covered in blood, and that the blood was smeared over his head and hands. He tried wiping it off on his jeans, but no matter how hard he tried the blood would not come off.

Yellow eyes watched him like a hawk as they began to circle around him. But before he let that happen, he sprinted again through the dense forest. His pursuers were very fast and gaining on him as he stumbled through the forest, trying to find a place to hide.

All of a sudden, he heard a young girl scream. In a flash he was headed toward the girl, intent on trying to save her from these beasts that must be chasing her as well. He was running so hard he didn't realize he had broken into a clearing that held seven people standing in the circle. He recognized two of them as his mom and dad. He screamed at them to turn around and yelled a warning about the creatures with the yellow eyes. But, they could not hear him. Then he saw a small girl standing in the middle of the circle. It was the girl in white. She was crying and begging them to leave her alone. The seven people in the circle began to move toward the girl with a madness in their eyes. They were going to kill her. He yelled with all his might but they could not hear him.

Ernie yelled and yelled but he could not get their attention, and it was too late anyway. The monsters with the devil eyes had caught up with him. They looked like overgrown wolves, but he knew for certain who those eyes belonged to, and he knew exactly who had brought the devil into their town. Before his eyes popped open one of the creatures was ripping off his foot, and he was still screaming as he sat up in bed and realized it had only been a dream.

Well, part of a dream; he was missing his right pinkie toe, after all.

Katie Barker
Katie was tossing fitfully in her bed. She hadn't been able to sleep very well while they had been kept hostage in the *house on the hill*. Now as she drifted along in a semi-fog, her head seemed to be spinning with images of her father in his surgical clothes.

As the fog was clearing she was up above him in the observation room, watching him perform an operation, which was odd because that was something that she had never been allowed to do before. She knew that interns sometimes watched from this vantage point to take notes on the kind of surgery that was being performed.

The patient was a young girl about her age. She had blonde hair and she was very pale. It looked as though they were performing some type of heart surgery on her, but it did not seem to be going well. Her father was sweating profusely and he was yelling at the other surgeons and other surgical assistants. His words were unintelligible to her ears, but she could tell he was really scared for the patient lying on the table.

Suddenly Katie realized who the girl was; it was the girl from the picture in her chamber room. The angle in white! She pressed her hands to the glass and tried to yell to her father, but he couldn't hear her. Because, she knew for certain that his patient was going to die. Katie screamed to her father that it wasn't his fault, but then she stopped cold as her hands pressed harder against the glass.

The heart monitor flatlined, but her father went into a frenzy using the paddles to shock her again and again. The assistants tried to calm him, but he would not stop trying to revive her. It was as if he could not admit that she was dead. Almost as if it was his fault that she had died on that operating table.

Katie woke from her dream with tears streaming down her face. What had really happened so long ago? All four of them in the chamber rooms now knew that their parents had participated in the murder of the angel in white. And, *The Reaper* wanted that to come to light. He must have loved her a great deal to bring justice to something that happened so long ago.

Jake White

The Middle Eastern Church rose above the other adobe-style houses in the small village in Jake's dream. In the town square, several men were digging a deep hole in the middle of a huge square of dirt that was directly in front of the church. Jake tried to get up to go and talk to the men but found that his hands and feet were bound together, and he could not move. He called out, but the men ignored him and continued with their task.

As Jake struggled at the ropes, he saw a crowd was gathering in close to where the men were digging the hole. Their faces looked barren and angry as they glared at him. Jake's heart began to beat loudly in his ears and he started to cry out for help, but the people simply looked at him with their eyes bent on revenge.

When the hole was complete, the men walked toward Jake and lifted him up. He struggled against them but it was no use. They took him to the hole and put his body in feet first. The hole reached up just past his waist. He continued to cry and struggle as the men filled in the dirt around him until his lower body and tied hands were buried beneath the dirt. The crowd dressed in the clothing of this village of long ago continued to gather, and it looked as if over a hundred people were now looking at him with such hatred; he began to cry and scream for help over and over again. Suddenly, out of the corner of his eye, he saw a few people in the crowd move over to a huge pile of stones. They gathered them in their hands, and as they did so more and more of these people began to gather the stones as well.

Jake heard a man reading something in a language he could not understand. But he didn't need to understand the words the man was saying. He was about to be stoned to death for a crime these people believed he had committed. Screaming at them to stop, his chest heaving, Jake awoke from the dream before the first stone hit his body.

Ryan Happer
Ryan wasn't dreaming. He was praying. Praying for all of them! Not just for Katie, Jake, Ernie Jr., and himself, but for their parents as well. He prayed for all of the people that had been so terribly hurt by what happened in the town so long ago.

Although Ryan did not want to face what his father might have been capable of all those years in the past, he knew it was something absolutely horrific. He knew it with all of his heart. So, he was praying. Praying for their souls. For God to forgive them all. But, most of all, he was praying for *The Reaper*. For he knew *The Reaper*'s pain must be the most profound, if he would go to such lengths to find justice *for the angel in white*.

Part Four
And Justice for All

Chapter Sixty-three

THE PACK

11:30 P.M. – All Hallows' Eve, Present Day

When the seven members of *the pack* walked into the police station in the early morning hours of Halloween, Reese walked toward them with a hollow look on his face. He saw that Ernie Johnson was beaten to a bloody pulp, and the only thing he could think was that he wished he was the one who had done the beating.

He looked at the seven people standing before him as Sheriff White's deputy emerged from his office.

"What the hell happened to him?" he asked Reese.

"I don't know. But, I expect we're about to find out."

By the time they walked into the office Ray had put the gun away. He told them not to say a word about the gun that brought them here.But, if they confessed to the murder their children would be freed.

Reese regarded the seven people that had just walked into the police station.

Sheriff White pulled the white letter from his pocket. The last one that each of them had received from *The Reaper*.

Reese read the letter and looked up at them. Ernie looked like a he had gone through a tornado. He could not help feeling glad about the fact. He was just sorry he wasn't the one who had the pleasure in being the one who had beat *the shit* out of him.

"We are here to give our confession of the murder that happened twenty-five years ago in this town. The murder of Madeline Singer," said Ray.

Reese stared at the people before him. So they were finally admitting the connection that all of them had as to why their children had been taken.

Reese and Deputy Martin set up the integration room. Readied the cameras and the listening devices. Then he and Alicia Davidson readied themselves for a confession so horrific it was hard to remain in their seats.

Then one by one *the pack* went into the interrogation room to give the account of the murder. The deputy had read them all their rights and all of them had waived the right to an attorney, pleading guilty to the murder that occurred twenty-five years ago.

Detective Reese and Detective Alicia Davidson taped their confession as evidence and as Reese listened to what they had done to his beautiful friend; it was all he could do to keep his composure. It was the hardest thing he had to sit through in his life.

Twenty-five Years Ago – All Hallows' Eve
The Murder of Madeline Singer
The pack chased Madeline toward the bank of the river. If she had only chosen to run in the other direction to a nearby house, the outcome might have been different if they hadn't caught up with her first.

But utter fear took over her whole body and she wasn't thinking where she was heading as she ran; she only wanted to get away from the seven members of *the pack* who called themselves *"the shit."*

Once she reached the edge of the water, she realized she had nowhere to go. *The pack* closed in around her. Their eyes glistening with pure hatred. She cried and begged for them to leave her alone.

The pack howled with laughter and as she tried to run past them, Todd Barker tripped her, and she landed with a thud on the muddy bank of the river. When she hit the ground, she cried out in pain, which only made *the pack* more feral in inflicting terror into the girl lying on the ground.

At first *the pack* just surrounded her, calling her names as she curled up in a ball trying to protect herself from the onslaught of emotional cruelty that was being delivered from five members from *the pack*. For Ray White could not participate in this type of atrocity. Madeline was his friend. Little did he know how much worse it was going to get by the time they were done with his beautiful friend.

"Come on, guys, let's go and leave her alone," Ray said in a pleading voice.

"Shut up, Gay Bait," spat Todd Barker.

"I agree with Ray," said Paul in a shaky voice, looking around the bank of the river.

"Suddenly get religion, Paul?" mocked Ernie.

The pack continued to taunt Madeline but then all of a sudden, like the turning of a clock, the madness took complete control of them. Ray saw it in their eyes and it turned his blood to ice.

The first kick to the stomach came from Todd Barker. Madeline screamed in pain. *The pack* laughed in sinister delight. Another kick from Todd, John, and Ernie to the stomach, back, and head. Madeline tried to protect her body with her arms and hands, but it was no use.

She screamed and cried, pleaded for them to stop. But the devil was with them that night. They had allowed him to lace his fingers into their very souls, and the choice of evil had already been made as they closed in on her.

The kicks continued from John, Ernie, and Todd. Ray White stood rooted to his spot, unable to move. He couldn't speak, and he couldn't stop them, and he could not believe the horror that was happening before him. He saw that Paul couldn't believe it as well. Ray and Paul locked eyes filled with horror.

Vera Tate picked up a rock and threw it with brutal force at Madeline's chest. She cried out in pain. Then another rock hit her. This time it came from Tabitha. Ray had never seen Tabitha's eyes so clearly demonic.

"You little bitch, with your perfect parents and your perfect *house on the hill*," snapped Tabitha as she got on her knees and grabbed Madeline's blonde hair and pulled her face back so she could look directly in her eyes. "You think you're better than we are, don't you, little princess? Looking down on us from that mansion every day. You make me sick. So perfect! Well, let's see how perfect you are without your eyes, you snow-white bitch!"

Paul and Ray both took in huge breaths. Now, still staring straight at each other, they still did not believe that the other members of *the pack* would go this far.

The pack continued to laugh as Madeline screamed for her life. Suddenly, Tabitha picked up a sharp rock and walked toward Madeline. She kneeled on the ground beside her and told Ernie and John to hold her down.

"John, let's stop this, brother. Jesus Christ, think about what Tabatha is going to do to her." He looked helplessly at Madeline pinned in the dirt between John and Ernie.

"Your twin run your life, John?" laughed Ernie.

"I run my own damn life," John spat.

Paul backed away from his brother, across from Ray, and watched the most horrific act of violence that they would ever see again in their lives. With their faces down, Paul and Ray tried to shut out the last screams Madeline Singer would ever make.

"No, please, God, no, Tabitha, please don't do this to me!" Madeline sobbed.

And, as Madeline screamed for dear life, Tabitha took the sharp, jagged rock and jabbed both of her eyes into each socket. Blood was squirting all around them as her screams filled up the night of All Hallows' Eve. Her blood was everywhere in the moonlight; it looked black as it seeped into the muddy banks of the Ohio River. Screaming, screaming, screaming, everywhere all around them, like none of them had ever heard.

But instead of giving them compassion, it only fueled their hatred of the poor girl now lying blind on the ground before them. For that is the devil's purpose in this world. To take away compassion and fill it with hate, doubt, hopelessness, and pain.

Ray began walking and, stumbling backward as Vera, with another rock in hand, smashed the stone hard into Madeline's mouth, knocking out all of her front teeth. Ray's ears were burning with Madeline's screams. For God's sake, she was still alive. They had tortured her un-mercifully and she was still alive—blind, bleeding, and in so much pain that Ray continued to retch until nothing came out but dry heaves. The words that reached his ears had haunted him to this day. Just before the final blow that killed Madeline, she called out to him for help in such a hushed tone that he could barely hear her words. She said, "Help me, Ray; please, help me." So she knew that he was not a part of the torture, but in the end he was not strong enough to help her either. Oh, God, he had been her friend. She was a real friend, not like these cruel monsters that stood before him. Madeline had liked him for who he really was as a person. She had always been kind to him. And the enormous guilt of not being strong enough to help her had haunted him for the last twenty-five years.

Then Ray heard them cackle like a hungry animal. The last words that Madeline would ever hear. Not a Barry Manilow song, not her mother and father saying "goodbye" and "we love you." Not even her friends holding her hands, telling her how special she was in a way so many others were not. No, not anything beautiful that she should have heard when it came time for her to die. They had murdered her and taken away the entire life she had ahead of her.

All Madeline heard was the cruel, cold voice of Ernie Johnson saying, "I am always the one that cleans everything up, now get the hell out of the way!"

When Ray looked back at the scene, Ernie Johnson had a rock raised high in the air. He brought it down on Madeline's head, silencing her forever.

"NO!" Ray managed to shout.

But it was too late. Madeline was gone, and he sobbed on the banks of the river until the other members of *the pack* told him to shut up and quit being such a girly-ass piece of shit!

Paul looked away, not wanting anyone to see him cry. My God in heaven, they had committed murder. No. He hadn't helped but he hadn't stopped them either. But, he had a secret that the other members of *the pack* didn't know. Not even his own brother. He was a Christian and he believed in God. He believed that Jesus Christ was his Lord and Savior and that the strong should protect the weak. But, he hadn't done that.

Because, for now, he was not a soldier of God or he would have found a way to stop Ernie and the others. "Take up thy sword..." kept playing through his mind over and over. He had stood there and let them murder a sweet young girl. He was just as bad as they were, if not worse, he thought to himself: *I am a lowly coward, oh, Lord. Please forgive me and what we have done this night upon all nights. My brother and I will bear this cross all of our lives. Maybe I will carry a bit more of the burden because I know my brother is an atheist. I shall bear it for both of us.*

Then *the pack* began to panic. What were they going to do when someone found the body next to the river with all of their footprints and evidence linking them to the murder?

That was when Ernie came up with the plan to hang her from the tree. Ray thought for sure they would be caught hauling a body through town, getting the rope, and hanging it from a tree. But, the plan had worked. It was Halloween and no one even paid attention to them. Ernie got the rope from his garage and they hung the body from the tree. Paul and John stayed behind to clean up blood and the footprints by the river. It was a sloppy job. But, it didn't matter.

The case was never gone over, there was never a true investigation, and nobody was ever found or questioned in the case of Madeline Singer. They blamed it on a "child killer" passing through town. And then they closed up the books, sealed the files, and put them in the basement with the other crates of a few other cold cases that would stay buried forever. But, none as gruesome as the murder of Madeline Singer. It was evident to Brian and Reese that some of the parents knew their children had a part in the murder, so they closed it as soon as possible.

A few days later, when Ray wanted to go to the police that was when Ernie had freaked out and pulled a knife on the group. He'd told them, "We're in this together, bitches. One big, happy fuckin' family. If anyone dares to tell another living soul, it will be the beginning of your end."

Chapter Sixty-four

Awakening

12:15 A.M., October 31st – The *house on the hill*

Present Day

Ernie Jr. had awakened from the anesthetic he was given, and he had awakened to something else as well. As he sat up and stared at the bandage covering his missing pinky toe, an awareness like he had never known began to come over him. There were secrets about the chambers they had been locked in that nobody else would ever know. Just them. Just the four underneath the *house on the hill*. Things they were able to share with each other. For it was their secret and their secret alone what happened in the *house on the hill*. He didn't want to be a bully anymore. Ernie had changed in that room—changed for the better. By talking to each other they were able to piece together what must have happened to the angel in white, Madeline Singer. They eventually remembered her name because of the stories that were linked to this house. And, it chilled them to the bone!

When he had awoken before he was in shock about missing a toe, but coming out of the drug used to make him sleep he thought about the friends he had made in the *house on the hill*. He knew as they did, that all of their parents had done something horrific to the angel in white, so he was going to be brave and face what and why this had happened to his toe.

He had read most of the books *The Reaper* had left for him coming to the conclusion that there is a choice in everyone to be kind or cruel. To be good or evil. To be courageous or weak. And, throughout these long days and nights being locked in a room in the house with nothing else to do but read and use the sound system that had been hooked up so they could talk to each other, Ernie Jr. had made a choice in the kind of man he wanted to become.

Suddenly, the room to his door opened and an old man walked in wearing a surgical mask and gloves. When Ernie looked into the man's eyes, he saw kindness and pain. The kind of pain that might have been buried deep for a long time.

The old man sat down on the bed and began to change Ernie's bandage. The man had not spoken since he had entered, and Ernie also knew this was because he was carrying a great amount of guilt over what he had done by amputating his toe.

"Not going to take any more body parts away from me, are you, Doctor?" Ernie asked in a low voice.

Doc looked into the eyes of Ernie Jr. and shook his head. "No, son, that is over."

Ernie studied the doctor as he changed his bandage. He could still feel the power of the pain medication that he had been given, and he was grateful for that, but there were so many questions pouring through his mind at the same time. However, Ernie knew that if he wanted any of his suspicions to be confirmed, he would have to do it in a way that would shock the doctor into a facial response, not a true question and answer session.

Like his father, Ernie Jr. had been born with a very high IQ. Unlike his father, he was growing into his good looks much faster, with his golden coppery hair and deep brown eyes with golden flecks, and he had been used to getting what he wanted all of his life. He was the quarterback of the Middle School River's Edge Football Team, made straight A's without opening a book, but he was also a bully just as his father had been. Although Ernie Jr. was not even one ounce the kind of bully Ernie Sr. was at his age.

"Are you in any pain, son?" asked the doctor as he pushed up his glasses.

"No, sir."

The doctor was finished changing the bandage but before he could rise from the bed Ernie said, "I've been doing a lot of reading down here. I think it has something to do with the angel in white." And with that Ernie held up the picture that *The Reaper* had left inside, the story of "The Lottery" by Shirley Jackson.

At once the doctor's face contorted into a look of misery and Ernie Jr. knew he had it right.

"So, Doctor, I think one or both of my parents murdered this girl when they were about my age. *The Reaper* kidnapped us and wants them to confess to the crime. And, I am also guessing it had to be all or none. Tell me the truth, it was my dad that held out so long. That is why you did this to me. Am I right?"

Again the doctor's face was a mask of pain, which told Ernie Jr. all he needed to know.

The doctor looked at him through his sad eyes and said, "It's almost over, Ernie, they are confessing right now. The door to your rooms will be unlocked very soon. And, you will be free to leave."

"Tell me something else, Doctor."

Wearily the doctor's shoulders slumped as he peered at Ernie over his spectacles.

"*The Reaper* would not have killed us, even if our parents did not confess to this murder, would he?"

The doctor shook his head. "No, he just had to make them believe that he would."

"Our parents murdered Madeline Singer twenty-five years ago. The girl who lived in this house. They got away with it all these years?"

The doctor nodded as he stood up and walked to the door.

His back was to Ernie when he said, "Dr. Singer, don't ever feel guilty about my pinky toe. You've lived a lifetime without your daughter. I think I can make it without my toe just fine."

In the shock of the moment the doc hesitated long enough to prove that Ernie was right. That he was indeed Madeline's father. The tears came to doc's eyes as he turned and looked at Ernie Jr. one last time before walking out and closing the door behind him.

Chapter Sixty-five

Scars

2:00 A.M., October 31st – Present Day

Reese exploded into the bathroom of the River's Edge County Police Station. What he had just sat through had burned its way into his bones. Before he could stop himself, he had smashed his fist into one of the mirrors and his fist came away bloody and torn. The glass was shattered everywhere, in the sink and on the floor around his feet.

Looking down at his hand, he thought of the scar it might leave but at that moment he didn't care. If it hadn't been the mirror, then it would have been one of the seven that just told the story that he had been waiting to hear all his life. However, nothing could have prepared him for the enormous pain that it had inflicted in him, right to the very core of his being. He was shaking so hard and his heart was pumping so strong. He thought it might just beat right out of his chest.

He and Brian had known that it had been *the pack* that killed Madeline. They had even tried to go to Sheriff Ray White Sr. after it happened, tried to tell him what they had seen. But, what they had seen hadn't been enough and the sheriff had tried to calm them down and let them know that they were looking into the case. That they needed to go home to their parents and try to grieve the loss of their friend and move on with their lives as best they could.

When Reese and Brian heard that the case was being closed due to lack of evidence, they were astounded and enraged. That was when they realized no one was going to listen to two thirteen-year-old boys who were blaming other kids their age for a murder that was so violent it would be incomprehensible to any adult they sought out to help them.

Sheriff Ray White Sr. and his deputies blamed it on a superficial drifter and closed the case as quickly as possible. But, Reese and Brian somehow knew in their hearts that they were covering up what they could not face. How could anyone face the fact that their own child was involved in the grisliest murder that was ever heard of in the small town, even though so many people knew that evil was lurking all around them?

Reese looked down at his bloodied hand and thought about the scar that might be left there, but it was nothing compared to the scars inside of him that continued to burn for Madeline.

Suddenly, the bathroom door opened and Brian Caster walked in and took in the scene around him.

"That bad," he said with such sorrow in his voice that Reese almost broke down right there on the spot.

"More than I ever expected," Reese replied. "When I became head of the CISVU, I had the files pulled on her death and read everything that was done to her before they actually killed her. I thought I would be ready to take that confession. But, it just about pushed me over the edge. I just wanted to kill some of them right there in the room while they finally confessed to the murder."

Brian walked over and looked at the bloody hand that ignited grotesque feelings inside of him just like the ones Reese was feeling.

"You need to get that taken care of," he said.

Reese and Brian had a bond that held them together since the night that Madeline was murdered. Reese was his oldest and dearest friend. They shared pain, loss, and sacrifice to lives that gave justice to the people that deserved saving and brought the gavel down hard on those who had broken the law. Both in their own ways, Reese in the criminal justice and Brian a prosecutor, for those that were guilty of crimes they had committed against society.

"My God, Brian, what they did to her! How in the world could seven thirteen-year-olds commit such a horrible crime and go on living their lives like nothing ever happened?"

"Because it wasn't them it happened to!" Brain replied, looking Reese in the eyes. "The abuser never feels the pain of the abused. Nor do they think about the pain it has inflicted in others around them. They did this to Madeline and went on living their lives. Only until the tables were turned have they felt that pain to the core because their own children's lives were on the line."

"Karma's a bitch," Reese spat, looking intently at Brian.

"It certainly is, my friend. It most certainly is."

Chapter Sixty-six

Manilow Magic

2:20 A.M., October 31st – Present Day

Brian walked out of the bathroom sensing that Reese needed time alone to get himself together. He told his friend again that he would need to get his hand looked at in case stitches were needed.

But right now, stiches were the farthest thing away from his mind. As he gazed into the cracked glass he returned to the memory that he had in his office before coming back to River's Edge. The day when he Brian and Ray had worn their suits to Madeline's house for brunch.

As soon as Madeline had poured the tea for Reese and Brian, the doorbell rang again. Madeline skipped to the door and they were astounded to see that Ray White had been invited to the party as well.

Ray's suit was perfect, and he had used gel to comb over his hair and slick it back. He had brought Madeline flowers—yellow roses, in fact. The color of friendship.

Madeline escorted him to the table and had him sit at the place setting that had been readied for him before the party began. They hadn't noticed that his name had been printed on a card in front of his plate as well.

To say they were shocked to see him there would have been an understatement. They knew that Madeline was kind to him at school. But they never would have guessed that he would be sitting there in the midst of the "Three Musketeers" on that beautiful spring day.

They chatted with Ray as Madeline put on her favorite music. Barry Manilow came out of the speakers singing "Mandy," and when she came back to the table her smile was so wide with happiness that the other boys didn't mind listening to her choice of music. Madeline's mother loved Barry Manilow, and when she was growing up she had passed that love along to Madeline. In fact, they almost named her Mandy, like the song, but decided to name her after her grandmother instead. The boys had no idea who Barry Manilow was, but supposedly a lot of women Madeline's mom's age loved him!

"His voice and his songs are like magic to me," Madeline said as she poured the tea for herself, and then they all ate the brunch that she and her mother had made.

As Manilow continued to sing song after song, the four of them talked and laughed. Reese could tell that Ray was happier than he'd ever seen him. They were able to see the real boy behind the one that "the pack" toted around with them. He even raised his glass of tea in a toast to Madeline. Reese and Brian did the same.

Madeline beamed with pride and joy for her friends. She thought of them as her family. Reese understood she knew Ray was a good person underneath the shadow of "the pack" and was trying to show him he could have other friends instead of being around the six people who constantly abused him.

Reese came out of the memory with tears glistening on his face, and he looked down at his bloody hand through the water that had pooled in his eyes.

When he finally had himself together, he walked out of the bathroom looking for Alicia Davidson and a first-aid kit.

Chapter Sixty-seven
Getting Out
2:45 A.M., October 31st – The *house on the hill*

The voice that came over the loud speaker was definitely not *The Reaper*, which meant he had a partner in this kidnapping. All four of them listened to what he had to say to them.

"Your parents have confessed and are now at the River's Edge Police Station. You will be released in a few hours from now. *The Reaper* hopes that you have used this time to read about good and evil while all of you have been allowed to speak to each other after the second day. How evil can carve its way deep into the soul. So deep that you never come back to the light. He hopes that you will make better choices than your parents made as they were growing up here in River's Edge. Your future is in no one's hands but your own.

"You will be out of you chambers in a matter of hours. He regrets having to put you in this nightmare."

Secret of the Four
The Reaper didn't want them to feel alone. So on the third day a sound system opened that was linked to all four rooms. They decided they would never tell another living soul what they talked about with each other in the last four days—when Katie cried and they tried so hard to comfort her, when they listened to the *Bible* that Ryan read out loud sometimes. It helped them fall

asleep. So, they read and talked. They began to form a bond, a compassion for the light that was beginning to seep in their souls. A great deal of the conversations would be hidden in their minds because no one would ever understand what they went through. When they all began talking and linking the information they each had about the *house on the hill*, a picture began to form in their minds. They remembered the name of the girl who lived in the house so many years ago. They also remembered stories about the girl being murdered on Halloween. And, then their blood turned cold as ice as they realized their parents were involved in this horrific loss of life.

Going Home
Doc turned off the microphone and walked out of the glass-encased room in which he had just spoken to the four innocent young teenagers that had to be taken for this plan to come to fruition. He donned his fedora, picked up his satchel and suitcase, and walked out of the *house on the hill* forever.

Pulling his car out of the driveway, his thoughts turned to Madeline. One last look at the house and he was on his way back to the airport. Back to his wife to tell her that at long last they had found the people who had murdered their daughter. For his wife had not killed herself as so many people thought in the town of River's Edge. They moved away very quickly because the pain was too hard to bear. But, the rumors were just another untruth that became bigger every time someone talked about what had happened in the town twenty-five years ago. A tale of gossip—no more, no less. But, it still hurt all the same. With tears running down his face he proceeded to the airport, leaving the past behind him.

Chapter Sixty-eight
Waiting to be Released
3:00 A.M., October 31st – The *house on the hill*

Ernie Jr.
Ernie Jr. knew who was speaking over the loud system in their rooms, and he also knew for certain the other three had no idea who was behind that voice. Of course, none of them had lost a body part in this whole plot to get their parents to confess.

He was not going to tell them who it was that cut off his toe. He would not tell them about the pain in the old man's face. No one would know that Dr. Singer had been a part of the plan that brought them here. Because throughout these last few days, Ernie Jr. had changed—truly changed. He wanted to choose the light. He wanted to grow up to be a good man and make the world a better place.

Katie Barker
When the voice had come over the speaker, it had scared her at first. She knew it wasn't *The Reaper's* voice and she realized he had a partner in this charade that he had won.

They were going to be released from the chambers. Her heart was beating a mile a minute. Obviously her dad had confessed to whatever he had done so many years ago. She never had a doubt about the choice he would make to save her.

Another thing that she did know for certain was that her dad was going to prison for this crime. She would not grow up with him by her side. It would be her mother that would raise her, and they would somehow try and deal with the loss of the man that they both loved so much.

Katie put her hands up to her face and sobbed. She didn't want to know the details of what had happened to the girl that was the age she was now. She didn't want to know what they had done to her because she knew in her heart it had to be horrific.

How could the man she had known as her father all these years be capable of murder? He was a doctor—a great doctor. And, he had taken the pledge that all doctors take knowing what he and his friends had done all those years ago.

As she had listened to what the man had to say to them about good and evil, she knew that this experience had changed her forever. Although she was a good person she would try even harder now. She would try to become a hero in this crazy world, and she didn't think she would be alone in this decision. There were three others that had gone through this with her, and somehow in her heart she knew it would bond them for life and they would all choose to make the world a better place starting right here in River's Edge, Kentucky.

Ryan Happer

He'd known from the beginning that *The Reaper* wasn't going to kill them. The man behind the mask had been forming this plan for a long, long time. To kill them would be murdering four other young people and *The Reaper* could not live with the fact that one young life had been taken so many years ago, so he wasn't about to commit the same atrocity that he'd told them their parents had chosen as their fate. They were just the bait to bring justice to the murder of Madeline Singer.

Ryan was praying again in his chamber room. After the man was done speaking, he went to the Lord in prayer. Again, he prayed for all of them. Their parents, Madeline's parents, *The Reaper*, and their fate once they were released from these rooms.

For Ryan the path of light was never a question. He had followed that path for as long as he could remember. His grandpa had preached of good and evil, and Ryan had already made a commitment to God and always tried to make the right choice.

As for the other three locked up with him, he only hoped that they had heard the message *The Reaper* wanted them to hear. He hoped they understood why the man had surrounded them with these books. Ryan knew in his heart *The Reaper* wanted them to learn the lesson of love and kindness. And the other three people in the basement of the *house on the hill* could only know what he had gone through while living out the game that *The Reaper* had played to win.

Jake White

Jake was still having a hard time believing that his dad had been involved in the murder of a young girl. He just could not wrap his head around it at all. They had murdered Madeline Singer The girl who had lived in this very house.

The person he knew as his father was kind, caring, and he ran the town with all the talents that it took to be a leader. He would not and could not believe that his father was linked to the murder. Until he was able to talk to his dad himself and ask him all the questions that had been piling up in his mind.

Tears slid down his cheeks as he quietly prayed that his father was innocent of this murder. It just did not compute, did not register with the man he knew. His dad was a great man, an honest man, a loyal man—not a murderer!

Jake thought of the other three captives that had been held captive in the *house on the hill*. They had been thrown into this situation together, and they had come to the conclusion that their parents had in fact murdered Madeline Singer.

Rumors about this house still festered. Now all of them had a very hazy picture of what might have occurred on the Halloween twenty-five years ago. They didn't know the complete story but they did know their parents were somehow involved. And, it made him feel so sick.

He just could not believe that his dad could have been involved in what happened so many years ago.

Chapter Sixty-nine

We All Fall Down

1:45 A.M., October 31st – Present Day

When Reese Stone and Agent Davidson were finished interrogating *the pack*, they locked them in the jail cells of the River's Edge Police Department. Every member of *the pack* confessed to the murder of Madeline Singer. They were interviewed separately and each gave the same account of what transpired on that fateful night.

From what the case specified, Ray White and Paul Happer did not participate in the murder. However, the fact that they were there and did not intervene or run for help put them in the category of aiding and abetting. After all, they had also been a part of chasing Madeline to her death as she ran toward the river.

Tabitha Preston
Tabitha sat in her cell contemplating the past. The injection that Todd Barker had given her had worn off by the time *the pack* walked into the station to confess to the murder they had committed so long ago. It seemed so unreal to Tabitha; she had put that memory to the very back recesses of her mind. The nerve medication Todd had given her all these years helped her to forget a long line of regrets in her life. The box that she kept hidden in the recesses of her mind was now open. Every part of the hideous crime they

committed came to the forefront of her mind and she could not put away the memory anymore.

She began to remember a nursery rhyme that all the kids would sing at school when they were all about seven years old. All of the girls would get in a circle and sing it to the top of their lungs and then burst out laughing when they fell down, which was what the nursery rhyme told them to do at the end.

There in the circle with the other girls was Madeline holding hands as they played outside until the bell rang to announce that recess was over.

Before the bell could ring the girls sang many songs, but this one in particular would not leave Tabitha's mind and she could still see all the faces of the girls as they sang the familiar tune: "Ring around the Rosy, a pocket full of posies, ashes, ashes, we all fall down." The girls would fall down in a heap laughing and ready to sing another rhyme to a jump rope that someone had brought from home.

Ashes. The pack had turned Madeline to ashes when they murdered her on the banks of the Ohio River. She shuddered at the memory that had now come back to her with no help of the tranquilizers she used to subdue that horrible night.

Tabitha knew she had done the worst of the damage to Madeline. The memory exploded into terror; she could see Madeline's eyes jabbed into the sockets and she ran to the corner of the cell and wretched over and over.

What had happened to her that night? Something had come over her and she could not push the fury away that she had for the girl lying helpless on the ground. Hate had consumed her body and would not let go until *the pack* had finished what they started.

When Deputy Martin peeked in on her, he smelled the foul odor emanating from her cell and told her someone would be in to clean it up as soon as possible.

Then he left her alone in her cell and Tabitha continued to cry softly. She whispered quietly, "I am so sorry, Madeline." But, it was too late to be sorry for what they had done to Madeline Singer.

Paul and John Happer

Because of the limited amount of cells in the River's Edge Police Department, they put John and Paul in a cell together. For a while neither of them spoke.

Finally John said to Paul, "I am so sorry for what I did. I pulled you into this nightmare with me. You asked us to stop that night and I didn't listen. I went ahead with what *the pack* wanted me to do that night and it has ruined our lives. I know that you think about that night all the time. Sometimes I can hear you talking in your sleep, asking us to leave her alone."

Paul sighed. "You never dragged me into anything, John. Remember we were members of *the pack*. We were *the shit* and thought we were invincible. As far as I'm concerned, we are all to blame for her death."

"NO!" John yelled at his brother. "I am not letting you go down for this. You did nothing to her. Five of us are to blame for what happened all those years ago, but you are not one of the five. You have a son to raise! You don't want to spend the rest of your life locked in a prison cell for trying to stop us."

"I didn't do a damned thing. I just stood there and watched it happen!" he yelled back. "Then, I helped conceal that secret for twenty-five years. I think I'm looking at more time than you think, John."

"Not when I am through giving my testimony in court. You are not going to prison for something you tried to stop. For God's sake, it's my fault you're here. It's my fault that Ryan was *taken*. I will carry that burden for what the five of us did that night, but there is no way in hell I am letting you take on my sins! You did nothing wrong, Paul. You even tried to stop what we were doing; and that was committing murder.

Todd Barker
Todd Barker was on the verge of having a nervous breakdown. As he sat in the holding cell, his mind was filled with memories of long ago. Choices made without any thought of the future. Now, the rest of his future would be locked up in prison, only seeing his wife and Katie when they were able to visit.

His whole world went up in flames from the moment that he received the first letter. By the time he knew Katie was *taken* he could hardly hold himself together.

How in the world did he think they would get away with what they did that night? The memory kept playing over and over again in his head and it wouldn't stop. The only other thought were of his daughter.

Todd began to cry. He cried for all the loss he was facing in his life because he really did become the do-gooder that he vowed never to become when he was thirteen. But as he grew, he did develop a strong empathy for others and decided he did want to be just like his mother and father. They were such good people.

How he wished he could take that night away! My God, how could they have done that to Madeline? She was kind and helped other people. But like the other six members he had fallen for Ernie's power. And because he had done so he would not get the chance to see his grandchildren and participate in their lives. He would be locked up in a cell far away from everything beautiful that could have surrounded him. Because he became a member of *the pack who thought they were the shit*!

And how in the world would he be able to explain this to his wife, Amy, and his precious Katie Girl? They would see him as a monster.

Vera Tate

Vera knew her part in the murder was unfathomable. When she was telling the story to Reese and Detective Davidson, it seemed as though she were in a trance. The words flying out of her mouth because she wanted this confession to be over as soon as possible.

As she sat there in her cell, contemplating her fate, she wondered if the others had told the Feds what had truly happened that night. Or had they come up with some lie that would get them off the hook and leave Vera holding the bag all alone.

But that thought passed in a hurry because she knew they would do anything to save their children. *The Reaper* knew what they had done. So, every one of them had to tell the truth of that night so long ago.

Of all the ideas that went through Vera's head from that night was the rage that was in her soul. She was so jealous of Madeline because of that damned *house on the hill* that overlooked the town.

When they cornered Madeline, she thought they would just put a scare in her. Make her scream a bit before they let her go. But just like the other five members of *the pack*, something evil had charged deep into her soul and she could not stop herself from inflicting all that pain on an innocent girl who lived above her in the beautiful house that glowed in the moonlight like a beacon in a storm.

Ernie Johnson Sr.

Ernie was pacing in his cell. He was still bloody from the beating that he had taken from Paul that evening. They had offered to escort him to the hospital to see if anything was broken but he had refused. He had also refused to clean himself up, so the blood was caking up on his face as the bleeding had stopped.

All he was thinking about was Ernie Jr. *The Reaper had cut off his toe!* And how right John was right when he had said it was one of them. And, when he got the chance he was going to kill Ray. Right now he wanted to kill the entire pack if he could.

If Tabitha and Vera hadn't inflicted so much damage on Madeline, she would be alive today. But because they had lost their minds and damaged her to the point of no return, he realized that the only choice was to kill her. That was left up to Ernie because the others were backing away as they looked at what had been done to her face.

Ernie knew Madeline was going to die anyway from the brutal force that had been inflicted on her face and her body. That was when he told everyone to back up and he finished the job that the other members of *the pack* had started. Of course, he was the one who had to come up with the plan to keep them all safe. It had worked for twenty-five years. They had gotten away with murder until *Ray* came up with this plan to make them confess.

Although Ernie Sr. truly believed that what he did to Madeline was a swift ending to a long, painful death, he considered the fact that throughout his life he had killed three other people. He had no remorse for what he had done, and he had gotten away with it every time. Ernie Sr. was a brilliant man, but it was safe to say that he was, and would *always* be, a complete *psychopath*.

Sheriff Ray White

Sheriff White sat in the cell like a piece of stone. He hadn't moved from the spot from where he sat since they had brought him to the cell. His mind was spinning a mile a minute. They had confessed—all of them. And even though he hadn't been the one that did anything to hurt Madeline that night, he still felt like he was just as much to blame for what happened to his beautiful friend.

Guilt. Guilt had become his friend that night and he bore it like thousands of stones piled on his back. *The pack* didn't know that he and Madeline had become friends. He had kept that to himself. He'd had a true friend in that sweet, innocent girl, and he had watched what they had done to her. He didn't lift a finger to help.

He supposed it was his youth that had paralyzed him at that time. The look in their eyes was something he had never seen before. *The pack* were a truly mean-spirited bunch, but he never thought them capable of murder.

When he had looked at Paul that night, he knew he was not alone in what he was feeling. Their eyes had met and locked on each other as the others finished off his one true friend.

Ray could not ever get the memory of that night out of his head. It had plagued him day in and day out. He supposed that was why he worked so hard at his job. To make sure that justice was served where and when it needed to be in River's Edge.

He was through thinking about all the ways he might have saved Madeline. Each scenario had seared itself into his mind as he grew up to be the man his father wanted him to be, but Sheriff Ray White Jr. had become much more than that.

Ray fingered the keys in his pocket. The ones that Deputy Martin had forgotten to take from him when he locked him in the cell. He smiled a ghostly smile to himself; it was almost time to end this charade once and for all.

The Pack

Although each member of *the pack* was reliving the past, they were also scared to death about their children. They had followed *His* words to the letter and were waiting helplessly for any information that their kids had been returned safe and sound. Except, of course, for one pinky toe.

The only member of *the pack* that had no stake in the children who had been abducted was Vera Tate. The only thing running through Vera's mind besides the murder of Madeline Singer was that she was never going to be rich. Just like she had thought to herself when the first letters arrived from *The Reaper*, there were no *Publishers Clearing House Sweepstakes* in prison. And, everyone knows you can't win if you don't enter.

Chapter Seventy
Living with the Pain
Twenty-five Years Ago, All Hallows' Eve

When Brian and Reese had separated to go and look for Madeline that night, Brian had started to walk up Front Street, which was closest to the river. Reese doubled back the way they had come to the inner part of the town. They called her name as they ran, every second filling them with dread that something terribly wrong had happened to her.

Reese had no luck as he bolted to the spot where they had left her, so he continued his quick pace through the other streets with sweat pouring down his face.

Brian ran down Front Street and when he got to the end he heard loud laughter coming from the river. He walked slowly down the bank and saw that *the pack* had Madeline cornered. They were pacing around her as she stood in the middle of the circle.

Without thinking Brian ran as fast as he could to get Reese. Yelling his name as he went, but it took a bit of time to catch up with him. When he told him where she was, both boys ran toward the river to help Madeline get away from *the pack*.

However, when they got there *the pack* nor Madeline were nowhere to be seen. When they finally got to the spot where Brian saw them with her, they found blood on the ground that had tried to be covered up with mud and stones.

They bolted from the river with a dread in their hearts that they had never felt in their lives. When they heard the first screams they feared the worst had happened to their friend.

When they got to the tree in which Madeline had been hung, Reese went into hysterics. They knew she was dead and they were too late to save her from *the pack* that called themselves *the shit*.

As the police arrived, Reese bounded over the yellow caution tape running what the police were calling the crime scene. But Reese and Brian knew better. This was not the crime scene. That was at the river where *the pack* had surrounded Madeline. Where she had nowhere to run!

While the deputies were pulling Reese away and he was fighting them with all his might, Brian felt the deepest weight of guilt come down on his shoulders. Why, oh, why had he run back to get Reese? He should have charged into *the pack* and saved Madeline on his own.

Brian could not believe that they had actually killed her. His heart was beating out of his chest with pain, anger, and a hate that he thought he could never feel. The hate he felt for *the pack* burned in him like a fire that might never be put out.

Madeline's parents were crying. Mrs. Singer holding on to her husband for dear life. Sobbing and saying the same word over and over: *Why? Why? Why?*

Everyone standing behind the yellow crime scene tape seemed to be crying as well. But it was Reese's screams that chilled him to the bone. "Get her down, get her down…. Oh, God, get her down."

When they finally got Reese back to his parents, he fell into their arms sobbing. Brian was as still as a statue taking everything as if it was happening in slow motion. From that moment on Brian blamed himself for what happened to Madeline. If he had only had the courage to storm in on *the pack* instead of running back to Reese for help, he knew she would still be alive.

Of course, at that time he didn't know that two other members of *the pack* felt exactly the same way. Ray and Paul had just stood there and watched it happen.

Reese blamed himself as well. If they had not raced to the end of Front Street and left her alone, Madeline would still be alive.

Chapter Seventy-one

Seeking Justice
Twenty-five Years Ago, Five Days after the Murder

Reese and Brian started to follow *the pack* everywhere they went in town that year. They listened in on their conversations to try and find something more to take to the sheriff.

They watched *the pack* toilet paper houses at night, ring a doorbell, and leave a brown package full of a dog shit at the unsuspecting neighbor's house. They talked about other crass ideas they had for the people in the town of River's Edge.

No one in *the pack* had mentioned the murder while they had been spying on them. Until one night as they hid in the bushes and they heard Ray White say he wanted to go to the police and confess to the crime.

That was when Ernie had shoved Ray to the ground and pulled out a knife. His speech to *the pack* was enough to make sure none of them ever went to the cops about Madeline's death.

The last words that Ernie said before he threw Ray his inhaler were, "We're in this together, bitches. Just one big, happy fuckin' family. And if any of you dares to go to the police, it will be the beginning of your end!"

Brian and Reese had gone to Sheriff White to try and explain what had truly happened that night. But he didn't want to hear it; he didn't want to hear anything that they had to say. He ushered them out of his office as quick as possible and told them that they were just upset over the death of their friend and that was understandable. Finding someone to blame was part of the grieving process.

Brian and Reese could not believe what they were hearing when Sheriff White made that statement. They had tried to tell him what they had seen, what they knew, but it hadn't mattered one bit. The parents of the seven members of *the pack* swept it under the rug, even though Reese and Brian felt that some of them knew exactly what had happened to Madeline. After all, Ray was Sheriff White's son and he wasn't about to go down that road.

The case was closed and stored in the basement of the River's Edge Police Department, along with other cold cases that had not been solved.

Chapter Seventy-two
One Phone Call
3:15 A.M.
River's Edge Police Station
Oct. 31st
Present Day

Each member of *the pack* was entitled to one phone call. Reese let them make their phone calls quickly after they had confessed to the crime. Family members needed to be made aware of the situation so that they could come to the police station right away. They needed to be there when and if the four young people were released.

Ray White Sr.
He knew it wasn't a drifter that had killed Madeline Singer. He knew that his son was somehow involved in what happened to her that night. Ray White Sr. was a smart man and he was aware that the six other kids that his son had befriended were a bad influence. He never thought in a million years that they would be capable of murder.

When Reese and Brian had visited him twenty-five years ago, he had turned them away, not wanting to hear what they were telling him. But down deep in his soul he knew what they were saying was true.

After sending them home that day, he went to the riverbank to look for evidence of the crime. He had found exactly what he hoped he wouldn't. There was dark blood that *the pack* had tried to cover up and also a huge rock near the water that had blood all over it; he knew this was the weapon that had killed Madeline.

He didn't know what had happened on that riverbank and he did not want to know. He threw the rock as hard as he could into the Ohio River and covered up all the evidence that could send his son away for a very long time.

The guilt he carried over what he had done was nothing compared to the thought of losing his only son. He did not believe for one second that Ray had done anything to hurt Madeline. In his heart he knew Ray was a bystander, as the other members of *the pack* committed a murder that was inconceivable.

But he also knew that Ray was with them when it happened, and because he was there he would be considered a part of the murder. There was no way that he could watch his son be taken away to serve time for what had transpired on that riverbank. His love for Ray was unconditional. If he had pursued this case, he knew that he would lose his only child whether or not Ray had actually participated in the crime.

So, Sheriff Ray White Sr. had closed the case as soon as possible. He had destroyed any evidence that could connect *the pack* to the murder. There was no autopsy done on the body thanks to him.

He knew *the pack* had murdered Madeline Singer in cold blood. They had confessed to the crime to get their children back. *The Reaper* had promised to let them live if all seven members told the true story of what happened that night so long ago on *All Hallows' Eve*.

His grandson, Jake, would need him now more than ever. Ray White Sr. would carry his guilt for the rest of his life because if anyone found out that he had covered up the case he would be going to prison as well. So, he steeled himself on the ride to the station. His grandson was a good boy and he could not fathom him growing up without his dad and his grandfather as well.

Anthony Preston the Third
Tabitha had called crying hysterically into the phone, telling him she needed him to come to the police station. She told him that she and her friends had committed the murder of Madeline Singer twenty-five years ago.

Mr. Preston was in shock. He had been taking care of Tabitha's son Evan since the kidnapping of Ernie Jr. Now, to find out that his daughter and his son-in-law would be going to prison was making his heart beat out of his chest.

He had already lost his son. Anthony had jumped off the building of the Preston Power and Electric Company and had left a note saying that the burden of his life was too much for him to handle. Of course, he had no idea what had really happened to Anthony. He didn't know he had been molesting Tabitha and that it was Ernie who threw him to his death.

All he knew was that he was now losing his only daughter to a crime she had participated in when she was thirteen years old.

It would be up to him to raise Ernie Jr. and Evan. So, he jumped in his red convertible and headed to the police station to wait for any information on getting Ernie Jr. back alive. Tabitha said that *The Reaper* told them if they confessed that he would be released. And, he wanted to be there for his grandson when he was returned to them.

Reverend Happer

The call came from John. When he told his father the news, he had broken down crying on the phone. Both of his sons had been involved in a murder and he had always known deep in his heart that they were. Somehow a part of what happened to that innocent girl who lived in the *house on the hill*.

Twenty-five years ago, when the boys had returned from their night out on Halloween, he could smell the river on them. He wondered why his boys would be down at the river while the town was celebrating the holiday.

Something inside him urged him to look at their shoes after they went to bed that evening. And, what he found was mud and what looked like blood caked on their sneakers. Why would there be blood on their shoes, unless....

He had gone to the hanging tree that night when word began to reach the town. When he realized it was Madeline's body hanging from the tree, he sought out her parents and tried to comfort them. He stood with them until the body of their daughter was cut down from the tree and put in the ambulance that would take her to the morgue for an autopsy, and then to the River's Edge Funeral Home.

When he got home that night and found the shoes, he knew that both his sons were involved somehow. He loved his children so much that he could not make the choice that God would want him to make. Instead, he washed their shoes clean, taking care of the evidence that they had been to the river that night.

After the murder, he threw himself even more into his calling as a minister. He worked day and night trying to bring the people of River's Edge to God.

He worked even harder trying to get his boys to accept Jesus as their Lord and Savior because he knew that was their only hope of redemption. When the boys continued to reject him and his belief in a higher power, he just prayed that much more for their souls. When their mother had died from cancer, she made him promise that he wouldn't give up on their children. He had kept that promise.

When Paul's son Ryan was born, it was like God sent him a light in the darkness he had been living in for so long. He was as close to Ryan as any grandfather could be and his grandson believed in the Lord. Ryan was his second chance.

Now that his sons had finally confessed to what they did, Ryan would need him more than ever. So, he prayed to God as he drove to the police station that the man that called himself *The Reaper* would let his grandson go, unharmed.

Amy Barker
At first Amy would not believe what Todd was trying to tell her. Todd was her knight in shining armor. There was no way that he had done what he was saying on the phone. She pleaded with him to tell her it was a lie as she cried silently on the other end.

Todd's father had walked up behind her and asked to take the phone. She watched his reaction to what his son was saying. There was no shock on his face. No telling his son that he didn't believe what he had done as a young boy.

When he hung up the phone, he told Amy that it was the truth. That he and his friends had murdered a girl named Madeline Singer twenty-five years ago. *The Reaper* was after a confession to the crime, and when all seven adults confessed to what they had done he would give them back their children.

As she and Dr. Barker Sr. drove to the police station, she realized her husband would be going to prison. How would she go on without him? She loved him and Katie more than life itself. How would Katie react when she found out what her father had done?

Ms. Tate
Vera's mother was more worried about who would take care of her if Vera went to prison. She yelled at her daughter for confessing to a crime that happened so long ago. She called her daughter a stupid cow and said that she would not be coming to the police station to comfort someone that was a complete idiot.

That didn't surprise Vera one bit. She doubted if her mother could even get out of bed, much less take the trip to the station for her only daughter. Vera didn't think her mother could even fit inside a car.

This was what Vera had lived with all her life. A mother that cared more about herself than her daughter that needed her desperately. So, Vera hung up the phone and they led her back to her cell. She would be the only one without a family member there to help and support her through this nightmare.

Ernie Sr.

Ernie Johnson Sr. had no one to call. Both of his parents were dead, so he left it up to Tabitha to call her father to come and take care of Ernie Jr. when all of all of the teenagers were finally set free.

He didn't care that he had no family other than Tabitha and the boys. He was glad that his parents weren't around to stumble into the station drunk or doped out of their minds.

Chapter Seventy-Three
Gone
4:00 A.M. River's Edge Police Station
Present Day

After Reese Stone had his hand bandaged and *the pack* had made their phone calls, he was feeling utterly drained. They were waiting for *The Reaper* to make contact or deliver the four hostages to the police station, where their parents were now locked up in the holding cells.

There was no doubt in his mind that *The Reaper* knew that they had confessed. Reese was sure he was out there watching everything transpire. Soon, they would have the four young hostages back. *The Reaper* had what he wanted: justice for Madeline.

As the families began to come into the station, Deputy Johnson and Reese's team did their best at calming them down. That was a hard job, to say the least.

When Ray White Sr. asked to see his son, Reese relented even though he wasn't letting the other families see the other six of yet. He wanted police officers to be next to the front entrance of the lobby in case the hostages were dropped off there. He felt certain that they would be, and they needed their families to be the first thing they saw when they were released.

Reese walked Ray White Sr. back to the holding cells and stopped at the one where they were holding his son. Only Ray White Jr. was not there. Reese yelled for Deputy Martin and asked him if he had taken Sheriff White back to his cell after he had made his phone call.

"Yes, sir," he replied as he came to a halt beside the empty cell.

"Did you make sure to take his keys before you locked him in here?" Reese asked.

Deputy Martin lowered his head. He had forgotten to take the keys.

Reese and Deputy Martin ran to the room where the other detectives were seated going over the cold case files of Madeline Singer.

"Have you seen Sheriff White?" he asked his team and the other officers in the room.

No one had seen Sheriff White since he had been led back to his cell after his phone call. Reese was frantic. He ran to Sheriff White's office and opened the door with Deputy Martin hot on his heels.

When he reached the sheriff's desk, he saw a white envelope with his name typed neatly across the back. Reese tore the envelope open and his face went ashen as he read the words that were on the paper. There were only five words typed in the middle of the sheet. It said: "The *house on the hill*."

Reese ran back to the room where his team and the other officers were sitting. He cried out, "The *house on the hill*, now!"

Four police cars pulled out of the River's Edge Station and headed for the *house on the hill*. They reached it quickly and headed up the abandoned driveway toward the deserted house.

They busted through the front door to find a man sitting in the middle of the room. He was wearing the hood of the Grim Reaper. He held his hands up in surrender and the officers pulled him from the chair and removed the mask. They could not believe what they were seeing. For the man hidden behind the hood was Sheriff Ray White.

Reese stared at Ray and he met his gaze. Shaking his head, he told the deputy to cuff him.

However, no one saw the shadow lurking in the back of the room watching the scene playout. So far back in the darkness where no one could see him. Hidden by the shadows with the hood covering his face.

Chapter Seventy-four

Released

4:30 A.M. The *house on the hill* All Hallows' Eve

Present Day

The officers who had known Ray all his life stood there in complete shock. They could not believe that Sheriff White was *The Reaper*. Yet there he was, standing right in front of them in the *house on the hill*.

"The kids are down in the basement in four chamber rooms," he said. "The key is on the mantle. It opens all four of the doors."

Deputy Martin handcuffed Sheriff White and led him toward one of the police cars while Reese and his team ran to the basement of the house and found the four chamber rooms just as Sheriff White had told them.

The first room held Ernie Jr., and when the door of his chamber was opened he limped toward them. He was having trouble with his balance since his pinky toe had been removed. He screamed at them to get the other doors open.

The next room held Ryan Happer, who bounded out looking around for the other three young people that had been *taken*. When he saw Ernie Jr., he ran to him and Ernie hobbled forward. They grasped on to each other as if their lives depended on it and immediately looked around for the two others.

The third chamber held Jake White, Sheriff White's son. He also ran directly to the two other boys that were clutched together. He put his arms around them and they all looked toward the last room, which held Katie Barker.

When her door was opened, she didn't pay attention to the detectives that had found them either. She ran crying toward the other boys and grabbed on to them, and all four fell to their knees holding each other, crying, all thankful, all linked together in the aftermath of what happened twenty-five years ago. What they had been through had changed them. They were forever bound by what their parents had done. No one would ever know or understand what had happened in those chamber rooms. "Because when you drown, no one understands unless they drown with you." They would walk forever as a group, not *a pack*.

Chapter Seventy-five

Going Home
5:00 A.M. The *house on the hill*
Present Day

Sheriff White was taken away in a police car just as the four young people were being let out of their chamber rooms. He said nothing after he told them where to find the four teenagers. He rode in the back of the car, hands cuffed in utter silence. He knew he would soon be interrogated for the kidnapping and he had to be ready to answer those questions.

Ernie Jr., Ryan Happer, Jake White, and Katie Barker refused to ride in separate cars as they drove them back to the station, where their families were waiting for them. So, Reese put them all in the back of his SUV. They held hands throughout the entire drive. When Reese Stone pulled into the station, he could tell that the four captives did not want to let go of each other. It made him wonder what had caused this complete and seemingly unbreakable bond between them. He smiled to himself. *The Reaper* had done his job well. *The pack* had confessed, and it was evident that the four he had taken would never be like their parents.

When they entered the police station, their families ran to them and hugged them asking if they were okay. Were they hurt in any way? Ernie Jr. was the only one to suffer a loss, and his grandfather was taking him straight to the hospital so they could try and reconnect his pinky toe, which was still on ice. Ray White Sr. told Mr. Preston to take the police car and turn on the blue lights and siren to get him to the hospital as soon as he could.

Amy Barker held onto Katie as she cried. Dr. Barker Sr. held back and allowed them to cry together for the loss of a husband and a father. Before they left for home, Katie ran to hug Jake and Ryan. They all looked for Ernie but couldn't find him. They all started to go into an anxiety attack when they did not see him. Reese called them over and reassured them that he was okay. And, they would see him as soon as possible.

Ryan walked to his grandfather and looked into his eyes. "I prayed, Grandfather, and I knew we were going to be okay."

Reverend Happer hugged him and then his mom, Linda, walked up and Ryan hugged her as well. They headed back to the Happer house to make sure that Ryan could get some rest.

Jake White was confused. He thought he had heard one of the officers say his dad was *The Reaper*. But Jake knew better. His dad was not *The Reaper*! As he walked toward his grandfather, he saw such pain in his face. Old pain and new pain but also happiness that Jake was returned to him safe and sound. As they left Jake looked back at the police station, where his dad had worked for most of his life. Although he knew his dad had something to do with what happened with the angel in white, he also knew deep inside they were never going to catch the real Reaper. He smiled at that. Jake didn't want him to be caught.

CHAPTER SEVENTY-SIX
FULL OF HOLES
6:30 A.M. THE PRESTON POLICE STATION
PRESENT DAY

Reese sat down across from Sheriff White, whose hands were cuffed together in front of him. He sighed as he looked at Ray. It had been the longest night of his life. Hard to believe that it was still October 31st. The hours felt like days and now he was taking the confession of a man that claimed he was *The Reaper*.

For this interrogation, Reese told Deputy Martin that he wanted to do it alone. The deputy was glad not to be face to face with his boss again, questioning him for another crime.

Sheriff White stared at Reese as he pretended to turn on the recorder and began to ask him how he had pulled off the kidnapping right under their noses. He didn't fit the profile that his team had worked up for *The Reaper*.

"Ray, how did you manage to lure those four teenagers to that house?"

"It was easy, they came to me," he responded.

"That's not really an answer, Ray. How did they come to you and why would you put your son through this kidnapping?"

"I've answered your question, Reese. They came to me. To the *house on the hill*."

"But why would those four just come to the *house on the hill*? It's been abandoned for twenty-five years."

"Well, it's like you said, I lured them there."

Reese sat back in his seat. "How did you get them down in those chamber rooms?"

"I wore the hood. I had a knife. They did exactly what I told them to do when they saw that weapon."

"Where is the weapon now, Ray?"

"I threw it in the river once I was done with it."

Reese looked closely at Sheriff White. He knew he was lying.

"So, you expect me to believe that you lured them to that house, but you can't or won't tell me how. Four teenagers? Including your son? You locked them in the chamber rooms as the *Grim Reaper*."

"Yes."

"Why, Ray? Why now after all these years would you finally decide to get *the pack* to confess to the murder? A murder that you did not commit. One that you watched but could not stop."

"I knew that if they thought their children were truly in danger they would confess to the murder."

"And how did it come to pass that Ernie Jr. had his toe amputated? You couldn't have done that yourself. You can't even tell me how you lured those kids there."

Reese leaned forward in his chair and looked Ray in the eyes.

"I know you didn't do this, Ray."

"I think I'm done with the questioning, Reese. I have confessed to being *The Reaper*. I have confessed to kidnapping them. So, I think it's time for you to make sure you take my keys before you lock me up this time."

Reese walked Ray to his cell. Then he walked back to where his team was going over the profile of *The Reaper*.

"I can't believe I was so off on this profile," Alicia Davidson said. "Never in a million years would I have thought that Sheriff White was the kidnapper. Oh, God, Reese! I knew something was bothering me and I didn't make the connection until now! Good Lord. The call to Sheriff White's phone was left on an answering machine. He is the only member of the seven that did not talk to *The Reaper* on that first night! It was in front of us all this time! Sheriff Ray White was the only one who did not speak to *The Reaper* directly."

CHAPTER SEVENTY-SEVEN
THE REAPER
1:00 P.M. NOVEMBER 1ST
PRESENT DAY

The man walked into Sheriff White's cell and sat down across from him. For a while they just stared at each other, waiting for the other one to speak. There were no listening devices, so what they said to each other would not be heard by anyone else.

"Why are you doing this, Ray?" the man asked.

Ray didn't answer for a while. He seemed to be searching for the right words.

"Because twenty-five years ago, I watched them murder Madeline. I fell to my knees and watched as they tortured her. I should have stopped them, and I am so damn tired of living with that guilt. *The Reaper* brought us to justice. His plan was one that he knew would work. And, I am indebted to him. I am not going to let him be imprisoned for kidnapping our children. He wanted the people of River's Edge to know what happened to her. He finally brought that to light. And, I am going to accept the consequences for him."

"But you've just added more years to your sentence. You know that you would not be sentenced as harshly as the others because you did nothing to Madeline to cause her death."

"No, I just watched, and I can't forgive myself for that."

"How long did you know where the kids were?"

"For a while."

"Why didn't you stop it? If you knew where your son was, why didn't you stop *The Reaper*?"

"Because I knew that he wouldn't really hurt our children. And I wanted *the pack* to pay for what they did to her. She was my friend too, you know."

"They don't believe you, Ray. They will eventually prove that you are not *The Reaper*. You couldn't have been at two places at once inside this investigation."

"I know."

"Then why do this?"

"To take their attention away. I do not want him caught for what he did because now the people who murdered Madeline will pay for what they did to her."

"So, you know who *The Reaper* is then, I take it."

"He's sitting across from me right now."

The other man looked closely at Ray. "How long have you known that?"

"Long enough to know that our children weren't really in danger. If I had thought for one minute that they were in danger, I would have stopped it before they confessed."

"You know, we have made it so that no one will ever know who *The Reaper* really is; we are in a position to keep that a secret for the rest of our lives."

"How?"

"Let's just say I have friends in all the right places."

"I know what kind of pain you suffered when Madeline died. And, I know you thought you could have saved her, too. That has eaten away at you all of your life."

The Reaper nodded his head. "Just like you, Ray. We share the same pain."

"Not exactly like me, but close enough. You had fallen in love with her. I saw it in your eyes when we were young."

"Yes, I loved her. *The pack* took her from me and my whole life has been leading up to this moment in time."

"I hope that now you might finally have some peace in your heart, my friend."

"There will always be an empty place in my heart. But now I've done what I set out to do when I was thirteen years old. I have brought justice to Madeline and her family."

"Good Lord, I wish I could take that night back," he said. I have dreams that won't go away. I see her hanging from that tree. But I was so weak then and scared to death of Ernie; it was like looking into the eyes of the devil himself. We feared him and he had such a blinding control over all of us. But that is gone now. Thank the Lord above. Thank you for all you have done over the years to get us here."

"You're welcome, Ray. You are not what *the pack* made you believe when you were young. You are a very strong man and don't ever forget that. Your son needs you."

The Reaper stood up and shook hands with Ray. "We have more than enough evidence that you are not the man who wore the hood. You should be out very soon. I will be in your corner."

Then *The Reaper* knocked on the cell to go and tie up some loose ends. He smiled at Ray, and Ray smiled back. Still friends bonded by Madeline so long ago.

Chapter Seventy-eight
The Four Musketeers and Their Parents
Present Day

Ernie Jr., Ryan Happer, and Jake White sat together with Katie in her living room. They had pleaded to see each other after they had gotten home the night before. Because of what they had been through, their families relented in letting them be together.

Soon they would be able to see their parents. They would talk to them about the murder of Madeline Singer, but all of them had decided that they did not want the details of what had been done to her. No one would tell them anyway because they were so young.

When they had first been locked in the chamber rooms, all of them were scared to death. They truly thought *The Reaper* might actually kill them if their parents chose not to confess. But as the time went on and they read the books that he had selected and saw the picture of the angel in white, they came to know that *The Reaper* wanted justice for Madeline and he also wanted to teach them a lesson about the fight between good and evil.

This was a huge step for Ernie Jr. because he had been and was already known as a bully in the town. Would he have continued down that road if it hadn't been for *The Reaper*? He thought so; he would have chosen a darker path for his life just like his father.

Of course, they all had a deep sadness inside of them. They were losing their parents. But they realized that path had started long before they killed Madeline. It began when they came together as *a pack*.

Now, they had each other. There would be no one else in their lives that would ever know what they had been through nor what they would be facing as they moved forward in the town of River's Edge. Everyone would know what their parents had done, and they would need each other more than ever when that finally came to light.

Light. It was there for them to grasp. *For anyone to grasp!*

The Thoughts of the pack
Tabitha Preston

Tabitha was pacing inside the cell that she had been locked for the last two days. Deputy Martin let her know that Reese had worked it out for them to meet their children in one of the interrogation rooms and that they were permitted to hug them and sit by them during the visit. She was so relieved that her son was all right. The hell she had been living the last few days since his abduction was unimaginable.

She was also beginning to have the shakes. The first sign of withdrawal from the nerve medication she had been on for years. After she had confessed, they had arrested her on the spot. She had been searched and was now wearing an orange pair of pants and a shirt. She had put her long chocolate hair back in a ponytail after the shower today and then spent the rest of the time thinking about what to say to her son. Tabitha had heard her husband screaming his head off earlier. She didn't even care what that was all about. She only cared that she comfort Ernie Jr. because she knew without a doubt in her mind that was something his father *would not* do when they finally got to see their son.

Paul and John Happer

Paul and John Happer sat in the same orange attire in the cell that they shared. They knew that very soon they would be separated for a very long time. They wouldn't be sent to the same prison, and John hoped that Paul's would be one in which criminals were held for shorter periods of time. As they waited for Ryan to get there, Paul was fidgeting with his clothes. His brother knew how hard it was going to be for him to face his son.

Sheriff Ray White Jr.
Ray White had asked Reese for a pencil and paper three hours before he was to see Jake. He had been drawing on that pad the entire time he waited to hug his son close and tell him that everything was going to be all right. Sometimes a picture can explain much more than a thousand words. He just hoped that Jake would understand why he hadn't been able to stand up to *the pack* before they had taken the life of Madeline Singer.

Todd Barker
Todd was lying on the cot staring at the ceiling. His wife and daughter would arrive soon. Thank God Katie was safe. At least most of his life had been dedicated to saving people. He hoped that would make up for being a part of a murder of complete and utter torture. What would he say to them? No way would he give the details of that night. He didn't want Katie to have the same nightmares that had sought him out night after night like a disease burning within his soul. Thank God *The Reaper* had kept his promise and let them go; his Katie Girl was safe!

Ernie Johnson Sr.
Ernie Sr. was still seething as he punched the wall in his cell. He knew he should have killed Ray White the night he wanted to go to the police. When the deputy had walked by, he overheard that Ray had confessed to being *The Reaper* and he finally lost his mind. He had screamed profanities and death threats so loud that he made sure Ray could hear him just a few cells down. Ernie wanted out of that cell long enough to finish what he should have already done. His thoughts weren't on his son; they were on the man he wanted to kill with his bare hands for betraying *the pack*.

Reese let Ernie Sr. scream for a good ten minutes before he came into his cell and took a seat. The hatred they had for each other was palpable. Lord, how Reese would love to beat this man into the dirt. He had to keep control of his emotions because if the dam started to break he was afraid he would actually kill Ernie Sr. right there on the spot.

"He isn't *The Reaper*, Ernie," Reese said in an even voice.

"What the hell are you talking about, Reese? I just heard those deputies say he confessed!"

"The confession wasn't true."

"Then why in the fuck would a piss ant like Ray White confess to being *The Reaper*?"

"Ernie, I know that as the leader of that *pack* growing up you thought you reigned supreme over all of them and many others in this town. You were thirteen then and a lot of things have changed over the years, more than you know. You aren't the leader of *shit* anymore. You're going away for a long time. Or, hasn't that sunk in yet?"

He lunged for Reese and in a snap Reese had him on the floor with Ernie's arm behind his back. Ernie couldn't move and was gasping for air as Reese pressed his leg into Ernie's neck.

"You listen to me, you son of a bitch," Reese whispered in his ear. "Try that again and I *will kill you* and call it self-defense. It would be so easy, Ernie, to snap your neck right here and now."

Reese finally let Ernie get up and he sat on the cot in his cell. He was rubbing his neck where Reese had planted his leg.

"Now, I am going to tell you this one more time. Ray White is not *The Reaper*. We have proof of that. We don't know why he chose to tell us that he was the kidnapper."

Reese got up to leave. "Now, shut your mouth; the screaming stops or we will transport you to another police station and you will *not* see your son today."

Ernie's rage did not subside as Reese left his cell. He did, however, stay seated on the cot with his mouth shut with his thoughts reaching into the dark recesses of his mind as they always had since he was a child.

Vera Tate
Vera's orange pants and shirt were too small for her. Her weight was getting out of control just like her mother's. She had called her mother again to let her know that she could visit. The phone was slammed in her ear. Vera's mother had no intention of visiting her. Most likely, Vera would never see her mother ever again. Not at the trial or the sentencing, and she would never visit Vera in prison. Her mother used her until she had nothing left to give, and now she was throwing her out like the garbage that was picked up every week at their house.

Coming Face to Face with the Past and the Future
The police station had scheduled the meetings with their parents at different times during the day. The FBI decided to give them as much time with their children as possible. Reese knew there would be much for them to talk about and explain. It would be hard on the kids having to look into the eyes of their mothers and fathers and see them in a whole new light.

The interrogation room was set up and ready to go for the visitors. Reese told Deputy Martin not to take the parents into the room in handcuffs.

"It will be hard enough on the kids as it was, but to stay in the observation next door and make sure everything they said was taped. I don't want them handcuffed until they come out of the room and are headed back to their cell. We're only taking them one at time to the visitation, so we shouldn't have any trouble. And, we will be watching everything behind the glass."

Deputy Martin cleared his throat. "Um, Reese, what about Ernie Johnson? He seems a bit out of control."

"Let me worry about Ernie Johnson," he replied, staring through the glass at the room in which *the pack* would have to look back into their past once again and talk to their children about what they had done.

Martin nodded and walked down the hall to the front of the police station. The first of the visitors would be arriving soon.

Ray White and Jake

Jake waited in the small room, where there was only a table and three chairs. When his father walked in, he jumped up and hugged him tightly. Ray held on just as tight. They were both crying, so Ray held Jake long enough for the tears to pass.

"Jake, I love you," said his father.

"I love you too, Dad."

They sat down in the two chairs next to each other. Ray handed Jake a tissue from the box that had been placed on the table. He looked in his son's eyes.

"I don't know where to start, Jake," he said.

"Dad, I'll tell you what I already know. There is no way that you could have hurt Madeline that night. I understand that you were there, but I don't think you helped them commit murder."

Ray placed the pad of paper in front of Jake. His dad had used a pencil to draw a picture of the angel in white. Although he had used no color in the picture, Jake knew exactly who it was when his dad laid it down.

"That's the angel in white," Jake said as he looked at his father. "There was a picture of her in our chamber rooms. It's Madeline Singer, isn't it, Dad?"

"Yes, Jake, it's Madeline."

They sat gazing at the drawing that Ray White had made for his son. "I thought this would be a good way to start to begin telling you what happened when the seven of us were your age. Madeline was my friend. She was a wonderful, kind person, and she liked me for who I was at that time. But, I was also one of the seven members that called themselves *the pack*.

"*The pack* did not value me as a friend. They bullied me the same way they bullied many other kids at that time. When they allowed me to be a part of their inner circle, I thought that it would make me stronger. At that time in my life I felt weak and to be a member of *the pack* was a dream come true, even though they treated me badly from the start.

"The night they killed Madeline, they had chased her to the banks of the river. Five of them surrounded her and began to call her names and tease her. I never thought they would really hurt her. When they were done having their fun at her expense, I thought they would let her go.

"When the brutal assault began, Paul Happer and I tried to get them to stop. But, neither of us was strong enough to save her. I had fallen on my knees because I could not believe what was happening before my eyes. Before she died she called out to me for help, but it was too late."

Jake put his hand over his dad's. "Dad, it was you against six others."

"Actually, it was five. Ryan Happer's dad, Paul, didn't lift a hand to hurt Madeline either. But, he was as frozen as I was to his spot on the riverbank. We had a chance to stop it, but something came over those other five like I had never seen before.

"Their eyes had a feral look about them. It scared me to the point that I couldn't move. She was my friend, Jake, and I wasn't strong enough to help her. That guilt has been with me for twenty-five years."

"Dad, you're not to blame for what happened to her. I knew that there was no way you would have harmed her, and I was right."

His father looked down at his own drawing. "She was a wonderful young girl, Jake. Madeline showed me a kindness that I had never known with *the pack*. If only I had jumped into that circle, I think I could have saved her. But I came to learn that we can't change the past. We can only move on with the future. That is why I ran for the sheriff of this town. I thought committing myself to making the town a better place would help me let go of what happened that night."

"Did it?"

"No, son, it has never left me. I am hoping that now that *the pack* has confessed I might be able to find some peace."

Jake began to cry. Ray hugged him.

"I don't want you to go to prison, Dad. You didn't do anything to deserve going to prison."

He put his hands on Jake's shoulders and pulled him back so he could look into his eyes. "I aided and abetted *the pack* by not going to the police. That is a crime, Jake. I have to pay for that."

Reese Stone opened the door to let them know their time was up.

"How long, Dad?" Jake asked. "How long will your sentence be now that you've confessed to what happened?"

"It won't be long if Brian Caster can help it, Jake," Reese said. "Brian is the prosecutor in this case, and he will fight for your dad because we know that he did not have anything to do with the actual murder."

Reese waited at the door.

"I love you, Dad."

"I love you too, son. You are my greatest accomplishment in this world and I am so proud of the man that you are becoming."

One last long, hard hug between them, and Reese escorted Jake back to his grandfather, who was waiting for him.

Paul Happer and Ryan

Paul hugged his son. "Thank God you're okay."

They sat down together.

"How are you, Ryan?"

"What happened that night, Dad?"

Paul sighed and looked at his son. This was what he had been dreading the whole time he had been locked up. Trying to explain to his son what had transpired that night. There was a part of him that really didn't know what came over his friends.

"Is this something that you really want to know, Ryan?"

"Yes, Dad. I want you to tell me that you didn't participate in killing that girl."

Paul ran his hand over his face. "I didn't. But, I stood right there and let it happen."

"Did you try to stop them, Dad?" Ryan asked as tears began to run down his cheeks.

Paul reached out for his son. He held him and said quietly. "Ryan, I would love to tell you that I fought for Madeline. That I ran in and tried to fight them all to save her. But that isn't what happened. When I was standing on that bank, I think I went into some kind of shock. I tried feebly to get them to stop. But they mocked me. I also tried to save your uncle from this crime. But I couldn't do that either."

"So Uncle John helped to murder her," Ryan whispered as he pulled back away from his dad.

"Something came over him that night. I could see it in his eyes. When I tried to get him to stop, Ernie badgered him. Asked him if he was going to let his brother run his life.

"I think that your uncle wanted *the pack* to know that he was strong enough to finish what they had started. One thing I am certain of is that he has regretted that night since he was thirteen years old."

"How could they murder an innocent girl, Dad? I don't understand why they would do something like that and walk away like nothing had happened. Living their lives while they took the life of another."

"Ryan, I was there, too. I am not off the hook for what happened. I stood there and watched them do the most horrible act I've ever seen in my life. Even after it was over I didn't go to the police. I knew what would happen to your Uncle John if I did, so I protected him because I loved him just like I love you. *The pack* confessed because we all love our children more than life itself. Your Uncle John loves you too, Ryan. Please remember, no matter what happens that we love you so much. We love you more than anything in this world. And, I am so proud of you, son! You have a wonderful heart, Ryan, and you will go out into this world and make it a better place. You are my greatest accomplishment. You are my pride, my shining pride, and I love you so much."

It didn't seem like very long until Reese was at the door. Father and son said goodbye until they could see each other again.

Todd Barker, Amy, and Katie

Katie ran to her dad. He looked her up and down to make sure she was okay. Then his wife was there and they all held each other and cried together.

When they finally sat down, Katie could tell that her father was in great pain. A crippling pain.

"First of all, I want both of you to know how much I love you," he said as he held both of their hands. "Katie, when you were *taken* I thought I was going to lose my mind. When the seven of us finally realized what *The Reaper* wanted, I was ready to go to the police that very minute. But we had to do it together, like *the pack* we were so long ago. We all had to confess as one."

"Dad, if you don't want to tell me what happened, you don't have to," Katie said, looking at the sadness on her father's face. She really didn't want to hear it because she knew instantly, just by looking at him, that he had indeed been one of *the pack* that had sent Madeline to her death.

Her father looked at both of them and hung his head. "I want to tell you what happened. I've carried the guilt so long.

"I was a mean teenager. At that time, I hated my parents. Hated what they did for a living. In my mind they were *do-gooders* and I promised myself that I would never be like them."

"But, you're exactly like them, Dad."

"Yes, after I grew up I realized that is what I wanted to do, to help people just like my parents had all their lives. I think the death of Madeline Singer helped me make that choice. I thought if I could save lives as a doctor that it would make up for what we did that night. It didn't.

"We chased her to the riverbank. At first, we teased her but then it turned into something horrific. I will not tell you the details of what we did to her, but I do have to tell you that I was one of the five that sent her to her death."

At hearing this Katie sobbed into her mother's shoulder. "Why, Dad? Why would you and your friends want to hurt an innocent girl?"

"Katie, the why of it is something that I can't explain; It happened, and I deserve to go to prison."

"I don't want to lose you, Dad. I love you so much."

"Oh, Katie, I love you too, my sweet, beautiful girl."

Todd looked at Amy, who hadn't said a word since they came into the room. She was crying silently. "I love you, Amy. I am so sorry that I am not going to be there for you and Katie."

The three of them hugged each other, holding on until Reese opened the door and escorted his wife and daughter from the room.

Tabitha and Ernie Jr.
Tabitha jumped up when Ernie entered the room. "Ernie!" she cried. "You're all right. They told me that you were safe, but part of me didn't believe them."

She threw her arms around her son and held him as tight as she could. Ernie hugged her back but let go quickly.

"Yeah, Mom. You got me back in one piece, and thank God they were able to reattach my pinky toe."

Tabitha sobbed into her hands.

"It's okay, Mom. I know it was Dad who held out and wouldn't confess to the crime until *The Reaper* sent him a gift."

His mother didn't try to make any apologies for his father, but she did ask him to sit down so they could talk.

"You killed her, didn't you, Mom? You and Dad both had a hand in her murder."

Tabitha looked at her son through bloodshot eyes. She nodded at him and he looked away from her.

"I knew it all along," Ernie said. "From the first time that I really listened to *The Reaper*, I knew you and Dad were two of *the pack* that caused her to die. I don't want to know what you did or how it happened."

Tabitha took his hand. "Ernie, if I could take back that night and give Madeline her life back, I would. I was ready to give my life for you if that is what it took to keep you safe. There are so many parts of the lives we lived that you don't know about. We were a horrible group of kids and we got worse as the years went by. I am glad that you don't want me to tell you what happened that night."

"Because what you did to her was like a horror show. Yeah, I already know that much from *The Reaper*. As I sat in that chamber room, I knew in my heart that you and Dad were one of the two that caused her to die."

His mother didn't argue. Just looked at him with her sorrowful eyes. "Be better than us, Ernie."

Then Reese stepped through the door and escorted his mother out of the room. Now, it was time to face his father.

Ernie Sr. and Ernie Jr.

Ernie Sr. walked into the room like he owned it. There was no remorse on his bloody face, only anger. He sat down across from Ernie and put his arms on the table in front of him. Arms that weren't about to hug his son.

Ernie looked at his dad and said the words that had been burning on his tongue since he had read "The Lottery."

"You're the one who killed her, aren't you? The others helped, but it was you that ended her life."

"I gave you your life twice in this world. The first time was when you were born, and now I have saved you from *The Reaper*."

"Yeah," Ernie said with his voice rising. "After I lost my toe! You were the one holding out all along."

"I saved you, didn't I? I did what *The Reaper* asked us to do in order for you to live."

"*The Reaper* wasn't going to kill us, Dad. He just wanted you to think that he would. And, he won the poker game by sending you my toe. I got it back, by the way, if you even care."

"I never thought he would hurt you in that way. You are my son, I love you," Ernie Sr. said, but his voice lacked the conviction.

"You don't know what love is, Dad!"

Ernie Sr. leaned forward. "I confessed for you—only for you. I am going to prison for you! And, you have the nerve to tell me what I do and do not know?"

"You're not going to prison for me, Dad. You're going to prison because you committed a murder."

For a minute Ernie Jr. thought his dad was going to hit him. His dad's face was bright red with fury. He never uttered another word to Ernie Jr. as Reese came to take him back to his cell.

Then Ernie Jr. broke down. "Dad! Dad!" cried Ernie and he ran to his father. He hugged him tightly. "I love you, Dad. I love you! I will always love you." He was crying hanging on to his father. "I hear you talking about your parents and what they did to you."

"What are you talking about, Ernie? I haven't had a nightmare in years."

"But, you do, Dad. You talk about horrible things that happened while you were growing up with your parents." He hugged his dad hard, crying and showing the love that Ernie Sr. had always wanted.

Then Reese saw something that he thought he would never witness from Ernie Johnson Sr. He fell to his knees and hugged Ernie for a long time. When he pulled away, he was crying as well.

He looked into the eyes of his son. "Then you are the only one who has ever truly loved me, Ernie. Throughout my whole life, you are the only one."

They held on to each other and cried. Then Reese told Ernie's father it was time to be taken back to the holding cell.

As they left the room, Ernie Jr. continued to cry out, "I love you, Dad! I love you! I love you!"

Vera Tate

Just as Vera had thought, she had no visitors. She watched as the other members of *the pack* were led in to talk with their families. For the first time in a long time, Vera was crying. This proved that her mother did not love her. Maybe her mother had loved her as a child before she reached the age of nine. There were some sweet memories of birthday cakes and Christmases past. But as time passed by, Vera's mother became angry at the world. An anger that eventually spilled over to her daughter. Vera knew she was loved by no one. She was all alone in the world, headed to prison.

There would be no letters for her to read from her mother or friends; she didn't have any friends since *the pack* split up. They weren't real friends, anyway. Vera cried silently until the tears dried on her cheeks. When Deputy Martin came by, she asked him if he had a copy of the *Publishers Clearing House Sweepstakes*. He looked at her like she was losing her mind. She told him never mind. He walked on down the hall, leaving Vera alone once more.

Chapter Seventy-nine
The Proof
8:00 A.M. November 2nd

It was easy for them to prove that Sheriff White was not *The Reaper*. However, he would not talk to them about why he put on the charade. The only one on the team that truly knew why was Reese. It was the hope of throwing them off the trail of finding the true Reaper.

Reese's team, along with the other officers of River's Edge, were headed up by his agent, Mark Daniels. They searched the house for clues. Any fingerprints that could help them in finding the man who seemed to be hidden by shadows. That was what hung in the air as they searched, shadows of the past and the present coming together. They found nothing that would help lead them to *The Reaper*.

No evidence of who he was, but the children were safe and he had brought to light what happened to Madeline. And for that, *the pack* would finally pay the price that should have been paid so long ago.

Reese closed his part of the case on *The Reaper*. He and his team were headed back to Washington. They were needed there, so they were leaving the town of River's Edge, Kentucky, behind. Deputy Martin and his team would probably keep their own case open for a while in the hope of catching the real kidnapper.

After the entire team found out what had happened to Reese's childhood friend, they had even more respect for him and his chosen profession. Maybe, they thought, he chose this life because he thought someday he would be able to bring Madeline's killer to justice. They had no idea just how right they were.

Chapter Eighty
The Reaper

Before going back to Washington, Reese met *The Reaper* at the River's Edge Cemetery. Both of them carried yellow roses to put on the grave of the beautiful friend that they lost twenty-five years ago.

Together, they walked where Madeline had been laid to rest. They put the roses next to her headstone. The yellow roses taking the place of the yellow crime scene tape that had been in their minds from the night of the murder.

Brian Caster raised his eyes to meet Reese's and tears were running down his face. "You did it, Brian," Reese said in a low voice. "Now, there will be justice for Madeline and her family. The whole town will know what happened so long ago."

"We did it, together." And, they had. From the time that Brian and Reese were thirteen years old and went to Sheriff Ray White Sr. to tell him what had happened to Madeline, they realized he wasn't going to listen—no one was going to listen. So, they made a promise to bring *the pack* down no matter what it cost them.

Brian became a prosecuting attorney and stayed in River's Edge, Kentucky, building his reputation. Reese became a detective. They both chose the course of their lives to "fight against the dying of the light."

When the plan began to form in Brian's mind, he and Reese made sure to go over everything together so that they could pull it off. Brian bought the house from Madeline's parents and waited patiently as the children grew to be the age that they had been when they murdered Madeline.

What had turned out more perfect than either Reese or Brian could have imagined was that *the pack* had their children so close in age, and that had been a huge part of the deception. The plan came to fruition; Brian and Reese both knew for a very long time that they were going to bring them down.

Brian had befriended all of them. Spent years having to be in their presence. His hatred burning more and more year after year. In his mind, he became *The Reaper* long before he and Reese carried out their plan.

As Reese and Brian walked back to their cars, Brian bid goodbye to his lifelong and forever friend. Washington was calling, and Reese would continue to solve cases that came his way. Brian would prosecute the guilty to the fullest extent of the law, which was what he said he would do when they found the evil that was gripping the town.

"I'll make sure that the court knows that Ray and Paul weren't a part of the actual murder. Try and get a deal for them so that they can go home soon."

"And the rest of them?" Reese asked.

"I'll go for the longest sentence possible. And I am most certain that will be granted by the court. Especially after they hear the tapes of how they tortured and murdered her that night."

"I have no doubt that your case against them will be rock solid."

"No way could I have done this without you," Brian told Reese before he got into his SUV.

"Like you said, we did it together." Reese paused for a moment. "I loved her too, Brian."

"So, I'll see you on December 24th?"

"Wouldn't miss it," Reese replied.

Chapter Eighty-one
Back in School
River's Edge Middle School
Present Day

Everyone in town now knew about the murder of Madeline Singer. The group of friends stayed as close together as they could while they were trying to go on with their lives.

The second bell had rung and students were coming out of their rooms to move on to their third class of the day.

Suddenly, four boys from the football team had Jake White cornered at his locker.

"So, your dad killed that girl, didn't he, fag?" one of the boys said while two of them pinned his back to his locker.

Without warning Ernie Jr. busted through the four boys and knocked the one of them to the ground. Katie and Jake were right there as well ready to help if Ernie needed it, although he needed no help at all. Ernie Jr. was as strong as he was smart. He rammed the boy who said those words to Jake up against the locker and held him by the shirt.

"You will not talk to him like that ever again! Do you understand me? Your bullying days are over at this school. If you ever dare to bully Jake or anyone else in this school while I'm around you won't get off this easy, because the next time I'm going to beat *the shit* out of you!"

The look in Ernie's eyes said he meant business. The four boys walked away without a backward glance. Then something happened that would have never happened before *The Reaper*. Everyone in the hallway broke out in thunderous applause. It seemed to last for a very long time; Ernie had never felt so proud in his life. This was living life in the light!

Katie was beaming with pride and she flung herself into Ernie's arms. Then they were all there. All four of them hugging each other with the kind of love and compassion *the pack* had never known.

"I just love all of you so much!" Katie said through her tears.

Ernie placed his hand in the middle of the group, and the other three did as well. They put their hands high in the air and said, "One for all and all for one."

Then Ernie swung Katie around while she giggled. When they dropped her off at her room, they went in different directions for their classes with the kind of joy that only living in the light could bring!

Chapter Eighty-two
Chapter Eighty-two
The Hanging Tree
November 20th; By the Hanging Tree, 2017

The town council had all voted to cut down the tree from which Madeline had been hung. There were many men who came to help and soon the tree would be just a memory.

Brian Caster felt as though this was a symbol of a town coming out of the darkness. They were moving on just as he had to do now that his life's work was over. He was so thankful that he would never have to see that tree again.

Just before he started to pull away, he saw the four teenagers that he had held captive in the *house on the hill*. They had come to watch the tree being cut down. They were all holding hands and he realized what true friends that they had become.

These young people were the future of River's Edge, Kentucky. And, that future had never felt so promising to Brian as it did today!

Katie Barker
Katie watched the tree being taken down limb by limb. Her long dark hair was blowing in the breeze and her blue eyes shined. She was so happy when she found out that the town council had decided to get rid of it once and for all. Her mother had allowed her to come and watch as the men worked diligently on the task at hand. While watching, a memory of "The Lottery" by

Shirley Jackson was running through her mind. She finally realized why that story was so important to *The Reaper*. If only one of them had gone into the circle with Madeline and spoken with a conviction, she would probably be alive today.

Jake White
Jake knew his dad would be so glad to see this tree gone when he came home. The prosecution was talking about a lower sentencing or even a plea deal due to the fact that his dad did not have a hand in the murder. Every member of *the pack* had told the Feds what had happened that night, and all of them had said that Ray White and Paul Happer were innocent of harming Madeline.

The group that he had become so close to since the kidnapping stood with him holding hands. *The Hanging Tree*, as the people of River's Edge had always called it, was coming down. And, with it a hope for the future.

Ryan Happer
Ryan was another one of the group that hoped his dad would be home soon. It was too late for his Uncle John. Tears sprang up in Ryan's eyes when he thought about his uncle spending so much time in prison. The difference between his dad and uncle at that time was the fact that his dad believed in God. Something that he hid from *the pack* and even his own brother.

If the tree was indeed a reminder of the dark past of the town, Ryan hoped that by cutting it down would let in the light. He felt it deep in his bones. The devil no longer abided with them.

Ernie Jr.
As the tree was coming down, it was harder for Ernie than it was for his three other friends. Although they were holding his hands, he could not get a certain image out of his mind. They hadn't told them the details of the case. But he knew in his heart that his dad was the one who hung her from this tree. Of course, the other members of *the pack* had helped, but his father was the mastermind of making sure they didn't get caught. In his mind, he knew his dad had lived a life of abuse from his parents. His mother had told him some of the story when he had visited her again.

Although it was true that Ernie did love his dad, he wanted to be nothing like his father. Not even a little bit. It even bothered him that he looked like the man with his golden coppery hair and dark golden brown eyes. He was strong like his father from playing football, and he got his very high IQ from him as well. But now Ernie Jr. was beginning to put the pieces together. Because his dad was abused almost every day of his life left him feeling sorrow in his heart. If his dad had been raised by people who really loved him, would it have changed the directionality of his life? Would he have lived a life where his high IQ was used for the light? And would he have grown into a man who could really make a difference in the world?

He knew as well that he didn't want to be like his mother with her perfect hair, clothes, jewelry, and everything else that money could buy. His mind drifted again to *The Picture of Dorian Gray*. When he had read that book, it reminded him of the picture of his mother above the fire place. She too had gone on with her life putting what she had done away in the back of her mind and pretended it didn't happen. His mother had lived a life of wealth, and continued that life even after she helped to murder Madeline.

Now that Ernie Jr. was opening his mind to the possibilities of his future, he wanted to do something great with his life. That was overwhelmingly possible since he was the person in the little town of River's Edge who had an IQ that was higher than his dad.

Today the tree was coming down and their parents were facing the consequences of their actions. *The Reaper* had justice. Would the man that helped them all see the light be able to move on now that it was over? Ernie hoped so; *The Reaper* deserved to finally have peace in his life.

Chapter Eighty-three
The Sermon
River's Edge Baptist Church
Present Day

It seemed that the whole town was packed into the church waiting to hear Reverend Happer's message. A large picture of Madeline was next to the pulpit. She was smiling that beautiful smile and she had a pink bow in her hair. That is how Brian always wanted to remember her.

He sat in the back pew waiting to hear the sermon that he longed for all his life. He noticed that Ernie Jr., Jake, Ryan, and Katie were sitting in the front pew. They sat as close as they could get to each other while they waited for Ryan's grandfather to take his place at the front of the church.

When he stepped up to give his sermon, he looked around the church at all the people that had crowded in to hear his message about Madeline Singer. He cleared his throat and began to speak.

"When we let darkness take over our lives and do nothing to change it, the mark it leaves will be eternal. I speak to you as one of you today. For I allowed darkness to take over my house when I didn't realize my own children had been seized by that dark force. What came to pass in this town would be constituted as the worst type of bullying imaginable. And my children were a part of a group of young people that called themselves *the pack*. They murdered Madeline Singer on the banks of the Ohio River.

"This murder could have been prevented if we had just looked into the lives of those seven children and realized what kind of bullying was going on when they were together. I am quite sure that they inflicted emotional and physical abuse on many others before the murder."

"You might ask me how these seven young people could be capable of murder. And, I say to you they were not given or taught how to be any different. We closed our eyes to the bullying. We didn't want to think that our children would be capable of such a violent crime. What we need to realize today is that this type of darkness exists in our world. You all know that from what you see on the news and read on the screens of your computers. There are bullies that live in our world who cause great damage to the people around them. And, I am not just talking about our children. Adults are capable of inflicting as much pain on each other as well. Until we can all see that being cruel to others is a mirror that each of us will have to look back upon our whole lives, I fear that nothing will change. Let this message be a warning and a blessing to all of you. When you choose kindness, you are choosing what God wants for your life. When you choose to be cruel, it will come back to you at some point in your life just as it has in our home of River's Edge, Kentucky. I pray that each of you leave here with the message that we all have a mirror of the past. You may look into yours and wish you had done things differently. Let today be the day that you turn that around if what I am saying is hitting home with some of you. It is never too late to change.

"As adults, we must be role models to our children and teach them kindness toward all humanity. For without us, they will be lost just like the seven thirteen-year-olds that committed this crime twenty-five years ago."

"We have also come here today to talk about the life of Madeline Singer. She was a beautiful girl with a kind and caring heart. I have talked with all seven members who called themselves *the pack*. I believe they were honest when they talked to me about how they ended up on that riverbank and let the devil take control of them.

"I also believe our town must take some of the responsibility. We closed our eyes to what was happening right under our noses, not wanting to look into the face of the devil that gripped the seven thirteen-year-olds who will now pay the price for their crime. They will live the rest of their lives looking back into the mirror of their lives with the consequences of the past. I have a name for this mirror: Hell's mirror—a reminder of all of our transgressions. This mirror is a reflection of our choices. Please learn from what has happened in our town. Let love and kindness fill your hearts just as Madeline Singer did as she was growing up here in River's Edge. Let her life be a testament to all that is good; my grandson wants me to say let her life be a testament to the light of God. Reach for that light in your lives. Before I end with prayer, my grandson also wants me to leave you with the words of a poem that he read while he was captive in the *house on the hill*: 'Do not go gentle into that good night. Rage, rage against the dying of the light.'

"Shall we pray? Dear Lord, I pray that your light will shine in the lives of the people of River's Edge. I pray for the parents of the seven children that committed this unfathomable crime. I pray that justice be done but that you will abide with the seven adults who were led astray as children. I pray for Madeline's parents, as they no doubt still grieve for the loss of their daughter. I pray for our town and that you have heard my sermon today with open hearts and minds. Finally, I thank you for bringing our children home safe and sound. Guide us as we move forward as a town. Amen."

At this time Brian saw the four young people that he had held captive place a red rose underneath the picture of Madeline. Red roses, the symbol for love.

The Confession of Reverend Happer
Present Day/River's Edge Police Station
Reverend Happer had called and asked to talk with Reese Stone before he went back to Washington. They set a time and soon Reverend Happer sat across from the boy who was now a man.

"I have something that I need to confess to you, Reese. Trying to live with it has bared down on my soul since the night of the murder."

Reese had not turned on the tape recorder. It was just the reverend and him in the interrogation room with no one watching from the other side of the glass. When Reese had gotten the call that Reverend Happer wanted to see him, he knew exactly why.

When Brian and Reese were younger, they blamed all the parents. They were sure that some of them knew their children were involved in the tragedy. None of the adults stepped forward. They chose to close their eyes and go on living as if nothing had happened.

"I think I am already aware of what you are going to tell me, Reverend Happer. I am not taping you so if you need to confess, confess to me. I am not going to arrest you."

"How did you know that I suspected them and the others for the murder?"

"I believe that at least three parents knew what their children had done. They didn't want to face it because parents want to protect their children at all cost."

"When Paul and John came home that night I found mud and what looked like blood on their shoes. Instead of coming forward I washed their shoes. Part of me wanted to believe I was wrong. The other part of me knew I was right."

"You know, Reverend Happer, that you are and will be the only parent that will come forward to admit this guilt?"

"Then so be it. Right now, I am only thinking about what I covered up for my sons. That is considered aiding and abetting. I am ready for you to arrest me for that crime."

"I am not going to arrest you, Reverend Happer. Ryan needs you. You are a good man who always tried to teach your two sons how to be good people. They turned away from that and it is not your fault."

"I think it is, Reese. I was the one who *turned away* when I knew they were involved in that murder."

Reese stared at the Reverend for a long moment. "Reverend Happer, what I want from you is to go on preaching the message of God to this town. They need you to show them the light so something like this never happens again. Preach the sermon that you would have preached if the town had known what happened to Madeline. Make them see the light, Reverend."

And, that was just what Reverend Happer hoped he did when he delivered his sermon to the town of River's Edge about Madeline Singer and the quote that his grandson was so earnest about: "Do not go gentle into that good night; Rage, rage against the dying of the light."

Chapter Eighty-four
The *house on the hill*
December 24
Present Day

Brian and Reese sat in the observation room at the top of the *house on the hill*. This was where they had sat with Madeline that last Christmas together looking at the stars.

Brian had begun refurbishing the house in which he now lived. It was beginning to look like the house that he and Reese remembered when they were younger.

Reese had brought a bottle of champagne and they were drinking it as they looked at the sky on this Christmas Eve. Most of the time they were quiet, letting the memories of her flood their minds. After tonight they had promised to let go of the past and move on with the future.

"If Madeline had lived, what do you think she would have done with her life?" Reese asked Brian.

"I think she would have touched the world with her light no matter what she decided to become," Brian replied.

When the clock finally struck midnight, Brian hit the switch and after twenty-five years of darkness the *house on the hill* was bathed in a brilliant glow. The white lights that outlined the outside of the mansion illuminated the town of River's Edge, Kentucky, once again.

Below
December 24th (Midnight, Christmas Eve)
River's Edge Baptist Church was just finishing up the midnight service when the first expressions of pure amazement began to travel inside the doors carried on the winter wind of the snowy white evening in the town that night. People began to rush outside to see what was happening that had everyone so captivated. When Katie, Ernie, Jake, and Ryan came to a halt, they stood in awe of the beauty before them. For they had never seen the *house on the hill* bathed in such luminous light. It was absolutely breathtaking. And, they realized that the stories about the house were true. That the light could be seen all over the town. All along the banks of the Ohio River. It stood like a beacon in the night for souls that might have gone astray. Like a lighthouse for anyone who needed a way home.

Katie smiled at the pure joy of the lights that were glowing above the town. How sad this beauty had been dead to them for so long. They lived in a world that could be so cruel that it cut her to the very core! Why? Oh, why, did so much hate and cruelty have to live in a world that had this much beauty to show? She felt Ernie's arms encase her and then Jake and Ryan's as well. They stared at the *house on the hill* and hoped that somewhere, wherever he might be, that *The Reaper* was seeing the magic of that house. The magic that light could bring to the world, to the whole world when good stood against evil. When people just stopped watching and started doing. When bystanders stopped standing and started taking a stand for what was right.

Reverend Happer put his hand on Ryan's shoulder and smiled. He had forgotten how beautiful those lights were. How powerful they could be on a person's soul. They were like fireworks in the sky that did not fade with a power all their own.

And, right now far away, right this minute, Mr. and Mrs. Singer would be opening a gift of light that the four teenagers had sent them as a Christmas present. It was an idea that they came up with on their own, and tears came to his eyes as he thought about how the Singers might be feeling right this minute, so far away from the light they had given to the town for so many years until so much pain had ripped their souls apart.

The Gift
Mr. and Mrs. Singer were opening *the pack*age that had been left for them two days before Christmas that read: "Please open at midnight on Christmas Eve."

With a shaky hand, Mrs. Singer pulled back the brown package and Mr. Singer took out a picture frame with a poem encased in glass. It read:

The Star

A glowing lighthouse
For ships gone astray.
Throwing out a lifeline
Helping others find the way.

To stand on their own
On a sometimes raging sea.
Helping to restore
Light and dignity.

Standing steadfast
Rock solid in the night.
There is hope!
Just look to "THE LIGHT"

Written for Madeline Singer: A Star in the Night!

By: Katie Barker, Ryan Happer, Jake White, and Ernie Johnson Jr.

Mr. Singer also pulled out a framed certificate that showed a star had been chosen and named after their beautiful Madeline. They held each other and cried. Mr. Singer walked to the mantel and placed both of them next to each other. They walked outside and stood in the slightly cooler air of the winter Florida night and they looked at the stars. "Those children did us a wonderful kindness, Mamma."

"So shines a good deed in a weary world."
-Willy Wonka (Gene Wilder)

Heaven's Mirror

Are you willing to look
In the mirror at last
Does it reflect a light
"A heart of future past"?

Is there a kindness
Shining in there,
A heart full of love
That you freely share?

Have you forgiven
The pain of the dark
That took away the light
When hope had no spark?

Are you forgiving
What others have done
That took the light away
And covered up the sun?

Has the light started to shine
In the wind and the rain
And have you found
That happiness again?

For hope is always there
For you to take
To fight against the dark
It's a choice that you make.

So grab on tight
Tomorrow is a brand-new day
Fight against "the dying of the light"
As you charge into the fray

Hell's Mirror

But how do I know
What do I see?
A broken part of Madeline
Lives inside of me.

There will always be
Dark and light
Will you choose
The one that is right.

For inside of us
They both live.
Will you shatter someone's life
Or make a choice to give.

Heaven waits to
Give hope in the dark.
It can be the way
Where hope lights the spark.

-DeAnna Davidson Lipps

Literary Works Referenced

The Picture of Dorian Gray ....Oscar Wilde

Something Wicked this way Comes ....Ray Bradbury

A Good Man is Hard to Find ....Flannery O'Connor

The Omen ....David Seltzer

The Lottery ....Shirley Jackson

The Tell-Tale Heart ....Edgar Alan Poe